Mr Virgil Mc Lagan

83

MW01098973

Lily Millett (Chandler)
Jan 9, 1877 - June 15, 1898

What happened to
Aunt Lily

What happened to Aunt Lily

Al Boyd

iUniverse, Inc.
New York Lincoln Shanghai

What happened to Aunt Lily

iUniverse, Inc.

For information address:
iUniverse, Inc.
2021 Pine Lake Road, Suite 100
Lincoln, NE 68512
www.iuniverse.com

ISBN: 0-595-31520-8

Printed in the United States of America

Dedicated to my mother, Helene Mecklenburg. This book would not be possible without her family knowledge. Her information and other facts obtained from books and newspaper articles of the period has now made this story possible. However, even with all these new details, no one will ever know precisely what took place behind the curtains in Chilberg's restaurant.

"Father never talked very much about Aunt Lily, in fact her name was seldom mentioned in any family conversations when I was growing up," remarked the elderly lady as they were walking up the slight incline in the old Colby Cemetery. "I only know that there seemed to be some big mysterious stigma attached to your great, great aunt's name."

"That's strange, since it was his own sister. And you never knew what it was all about?"

The gray haired lady used the question as an excuse to stop and catch her breath. "Not really. Oh, there were hints and innuendoes that I gathered over the years, mostly occasional tidbits about her boy friends and the wild way they said she lived." She regained her breath and continued up the grassy slope. "It's a shame how they've let this cemetery deteriorate. The grass is so deep in places that you can hardly read some of the tombstones." She paused again, "Have you noticed that all the writing is on the upper side of these headstones?"

"No, what is the reason for that?"

"See the old road at the top of this slope that runs along the crest of the knoll?"

"Yes."

"Well, from that road at one time, you could look down and read all the headstones. It made it a lot easier for people to find the markers they were looking for because all the engravings appeared on the same side." The two continued walking upward. "Your great, great aunt's grave is on the other side of this hill."

"Did you ever get to meet her?"

The older woman stopped and tried to straightened her stooped shoulders. "Oh no. It all happened before my time. I remember relatives coming by the house and talking about it in the back rooms though." She glanced towards the sky then continued up the hillside. "It appears that it is going to rain again. I swear this has been one of the wettest springs we have ever had. My garden has just about been washed away, and what has not washed away, I'm afraid will rot in the ground from all this moisture." She turned to look at the young woman with her, "Oh, I'm sorry. Getting back to Aunt Lily, I know she kept a diary."

"She did! Do you have it?"

1

"No I don't. The last I heard, her childhood friend and neighbor, Anna Baker had it, but I think Anna moved to eastern Washington and I know she died after World War Two. I think it was in nineteen forty-seven, but I'm not sure."

"I'd sure like to get hold of that diary. Have you any idea who might have it?"

"No, none at all. I doubt if it even still exists. After all, it's been over a hundred years ago, but I did get to read it once."

"Really!" The young woman was stunned. "You saw it and read it! What did it say? Do you remember? Could you tell me what was in it?"

The gray haired lady stopped and rested again. "I think I can. The whole thing seemed so traumatic at the time, so when I read the diary, her story really made a long lasting impression."

"Could you please tell me as best you can remember, and don't leave anything out, including the murders."

"Let's walk over to that old viewing bench. Let me sit down and I'll try to remember and sort it out for you."

They both sat down and the older woman got a far away look in her eyes as she began. "Mm, mm, let's see. Aunt Lily, Aunt Lily......"

Thus began the story:

◆　　　◆　　　◆

Lily Millett sat up in bed, still tired and sleepy, stretched and tried to awaken to begin the day. Slowly she started dressing for work. As she looked out through the faded curtains she suddenly realized it was later than she thought. "Damn, Frank was supposed to wake me," she said aloud as she hurriedly slipped on the clean, but well worn white dress she had laid out the night before. She glanced in the mirror to brush out her long auburn hair, put on and tied up the high top shoes of the period, then rushed down to their small kitchen. "Mother, where's Frank? He was supposed to wake me!"

Jennie Bell Millett turned and sat the hot tea kettle back on the wood stove, "Your brother left early this morning to help your father cut fence posts at the Nielsen's."

"Now, I'm going to be late for work! And you know how upset Mr. Howell gets when I'm late!"

"We need to talk about that young lady. You're only sixteen. Too young to work at that rowdy restaurant of his. Only riffraff come in there."

"Oh Mother, that's not true. A lot of Tacoma business owners come in there for breakfast, or coffee and read the morning paper before going to work. And there are the early morning travelers too!" She added as she glanced at the clock on the counter, "Oh damn it! It's quarter to six!"

"Don't argue with me and don't talk like that in this house!"

Lily ignored her mother as she turned and grabbed her long black coat off the coat rack by the door. "I've got to go now," said Lily as she ran out the door and let it slam behind her. She still heard her mother voice, "We'll talk about this later, when your father gets home."

The chunky and unshaven Rosco Howell was busy making the coffee as Lily burst though the back door of Rosco's Restaurant. "I see you're late again! One more time, and don't even bother to come in!"

The smell of fresh cinnamon rolls and biscuits permeated the air as Lily tossed her coat on the counter top, grabbed one of the aprons from underneath and put it on. "I'm sorry, my brother was supposed to wake me, and..."

"Look, that's your problem! Not mine," Rosco angrily cut in. "Your job is to be here at six every Saturday morning. Remember there are lots of other young women who would like to have this job!"

"I'm sorry it won't happen again." Lily knew better than to argue. Even though the job was only for evenings after school and Saturdays, she appreciated the income that allowed her extras like new clothes, hair styling and cosmetics. Cosmetics that her mother and father always frowned on.

Rosco continued, "Just don't be late again!"

At that moment the front door opened and in came the first customer of the day, Mr. Tendick of Tendick Hardware. Rosco wiped his hands on his already soiled apron and turned his attention to one of his best customers. "Good morning Mr. Tendick. I have your fresh hot coffee right here. Your two pancakes, just the way you want them, will be ready in a minute or two."

Mr. Tendick murmured a low 'thank you' as he sat down at the counter, opened up the Daily Ledger newspaper, and began to sip at the hot coffee.

Two more men entered as Lily picked up an unlined, homemade order pad, found a pencil from under the counter and went to wait on them. They were both tug boat owners who made their living on the waterways of Puget Sound. Later some of the sailors, and 'wharf rats' who worked on the docks, would be coming in for breakfast as well.

Things will get better, Lily thought. Perhaps that handsome Ben Chandler will come in, and he would really brighten up the day.

It had begun to rain and it drove more customers than usual into the small corner restaurant to get out of the inclement weather. Lily was quite able to handle this small rush as most would just order coffee or tea to drink while waiting for the rain to let up, although a few of them ordered a sweet roll or a still warm biscuit to go along with their drinks.

"I've worked all up and down this coast, and all it ever does here is rain," complained Jon Engstrom who worked as a logger. "Got my wagon stuck in a swamp out in Parkland yesterday. Took me damn near all day to get it out of the mud."

"How did you finally get it out?" asked his companion sitting nearby.

"Had to get help from a farmer who had a team of oxen. Even then we had one hell'va time. Took most of the day. Needless to say I didn't get any logs delivered to Swanson's mill. Sure as hell didn't even make a wooden nickel, that's for sure!"

A dapper man of about forty traveling with a rounding brunette spoke up. "You think this Tacoma area is bad for rain, my wife and I just came back from Juneau, Alaska. You not only get the rain up there, but it also gets colder than the hubs of hell, with icy snow too. At least down here, it's just rain."

Gradually the rain began to let up and the customers slowly drifted out to continue their travels and other endeavors. During this lull Lily and Rosco began to prepare for the noon rush. Lily cleaned and wiped down the tables and counter tops, then filled salt and pepper shakers and checked the silverware. Grabbing a well used broom she quickly swept some of the still wet dirt and mud from the floor even though it was a losing proposition. She knew the lunch crowd would promptly track the place up again.

Rosco was busy in the kitchen preparing for the influx of hungry noontime workers. He was happy with the day's receipts so far. The rain was obviously bad for some, but it brought him a little extra income for the day. 'Beautiful weather', he thought to himself.

Soon the lunch crowd began to appear. Four men from Swanson's mill, still partially covered with sawdust, were the first. Then a short, dark haired and fragile looking young man wearing glasses came in. He was the stock boy who worked at Tendick's Hardware around the corner. Others now came in rapid order until the little restaurant was packed and Lily was hard pressed to wait on all the customers.

The diners were somewhat of a raucous crowd today, perhaps because it was Saturday and their spirits were higher than normal.

"Hey Lily, we need more coffee over here! How about a towel for my sloppy friend here! A bib might be better," remarked another. "Hey, where's my food? You guys are getting slower and slower." On and on the comments went, but Lily was learning to field them with quick retort and a pouty smile. She was also learning how to handle rough men, even at her young age.

Finally the noon crowd began to diminish, and they began to clean up from the small rush. They knew that customers would continue to drift in, but by closing time at six on Saturday evenings, Rosco's eatery would be almost deserted.

A little after four in the afternoon a handsome man in his early twenties entered. It was Ben Chandler and when Lily saw him her heart gave a flutter.

"Hi little girl. Say, you are looking cuter each day," said Ben as he took off his well worn black hat and laid it on the counter. "How's the coffee? Still decent?"

Lily stared at his curly brown hair magnificently combed back along the sides of his head. "It's still good. I just had some and it was okay."

"Great, I'll have a cup and give me one of Rosco's rolls if there's any left." He turned his attention towards the kitchen and yelled, "Say Rosco, are you still crying poverty?"

The swarthy cook, soiled and sweaty from the long day, poked his head through the open doorway. "Hey, it's not easy running a place like this. You try getting up at five a.m. and working every day until eight in the evening, then tell me how rich you are!"

Ben quickly answered back, "Yeah, but you get off early on Saturdays and than you get all of Sundays off. What a racket you have. I'll bet you own half of the Fidelity Bank down the street."

There was no reply as Rosco abruptly stepped back out of sight into the kitchen. He didn't feel that his financial picture was anyone's business but his own.

Lily set the hot coffee and one of the last rolls down in front of Ben as he looked up and said, "By golly, you are cuter than a bug's ear!"

Lily's heart leaped again, but she was careful not to show it. How she enjoyed it when Ben would come into the restaurant. He always had a quick smile, a nice compliment for her, and he wasn't afraid of saying anything to Rosco. Things she couldn't say without losing her job. She pushed her long hair back and tried to continue the light conversation. "So, how was work today at the freight company?"

"Oh, about the same as every other day," he replied rather nonchalantly. "Freight comes in and freight goes out."

She caught the lack of depth in his answer and moved further down the counter to remove some dirty dishes. Two men had just left and she was pleasantly surprised to see that someone had left her a nickel tip. It would help stretch the two dollar salary she made on Saturdays, and add to the fifty cents she made each week night after school. Four fifty a week, plus tips. It wasn't great. Most of the men who worked as laborers made about seventeen dollars for a whole week.

It was simply part of the discrimination that existed between men and women's wages at the time. Someday she dreamed of making a lot more.

She glanced at the clock on the shelf and saw that it was nearing five. With luck she might be able to get away from the restaurant by six twenty, that is if she had everything cleaned and swept up to suit Rosco.

Ben pushed his coffee mug back on the counter, dug in his trouser pockets and left fifteen cents for the coffee and roll. "Got to go and get ready for the Farmer's dance tonight on McKinley Hill. Probably see you all on Monday."

As he went out the door, Lily felt cheated because she wasn't going to the dance. Even if she had been asked, she knew her parents would not let her attend such a 'wild affair'. It infuriated her as she he was sixteen years old and not totally unfamiliar with the opposite sex. It seemed so unfair!

Rosco continued with the Saturday evening cleanup. Anything that could not be saved for the opening of business again on Monday was dumped out. Pots and pans were scrubbed, and dishes washed. From behind the counter he called out, "Lily, there's a little bit of stew left. If you want some, grab a bowl." She quickly ate the last of the stew, then helped with the remaining dishes. The restaurant cleanup was finally completed and shortly after six thirty she left the small cafe. Rosco, with the days receipts tucked under his arm in a small wooden box, locked and bolted the back door as he followed her outside into the dim light of the fading day. Rain from earlier that morning, mixed with mud, still lingered in the many potholes.

Lily took the last 'hay burner special' of Saturday evening, which was a fourteen passenger, faded yellow horse drawn trolley. It picked her up just a block from Rosco's Restaurant. A new rail trolley system was partially completed, but so far it only traversed along the main street of Pacific Avenue. Mayor Jefferies promised that the new contractor on the job would have the new system extended into the Hilltop area and south to the McKinley Hill district by the end of the following year. Almost everyone was eagerly looking forward to the new rail system. It was far more comfortable and certainly cleaner than the horse drawn system which left copious amounts of manure in the roadways.

For Lily, it had been a long day and she tried to ease her sore feet as she sat on one of the hard wooden benches in the old trolley car which still had traces of the original red upholstery. She got off at Jake's Corner and walked along the rough roadway, being carefully to dodge the mud holes. Light from kerosene lanterns was beginning to show from a few nondescript wooden homes along the way. When she passed by the Baker house she could see a dim light shining through the tall front windows and wondered if her best friend, Anna Baker, was home.

She continued past the Baker's house and walked up the graveled pathway towards her unpainted, rough sided home and opened the front door to the aroma of freshly baked bread.

Jennie Bell looked out from the kitchen, her flowered apron covered with traces of white flour that seemed to match the beginnings of the gray in her hair. "It's about time you got home," she admonished. "Hang up your coat and come into the kitchen. Your father has something to say to you!"

George Jefferson Millett was sitting at the kitchen table, his reading glasses down on the end of his nose. He looked up from the family Bible he had been reading. He pushed his chair back from the old round kitchen table and ordered. "Lily sit down."

Silently Lily did as her father commanded.

George leaned back, his right hand inside the top of his bib overalls. "You know that rough language is not permitted in this house. Anything disrespectful like that outburst with your mother this morning will not be tolerated. You know it is your responsibility to get up and get to work on time, and no one else's. We told you that when we allowed you to take that job at Rosco's. It is not your brother's duty to wake you up. Frank has his chores to do just like everyone else around here. Do I make myself clear?"

She had almost forgotten her little outburst earlier that morning, and certainly hoped that her mother would have let it pass, but obviously she had not. "Yes Father," she replied.

"The devil himself will consume you if you cannot keep a civil tongue in your head like any other polite young lady."

"Yes Father," she replied though gritted teeth.

His face darkened, "Now you will take this Bible up to your room and read James, Chapter 3. Then tomorrow morning at church you will pray for the Lord's forgiveness."

The color began to rise on Lily's neck as she softly replied again, "Yes Father." Obediently she rose and took the well worn Bible which he handed her and started up the stairs. She knew there would be no warm meal for her tonight. The aroma of the freshly baked bread still lingered in the air and she was glad she had eaten the last of the stew at Rosco's, but still tears came to her eyes.

George Millett was an elder in the church and a stern father. Together with Jennie Bell's rigid New York upbringing they tolerated very little. Sunday church was a must. Hard work was the expected norm and it was slowly becoming a choking collar around the neck of the young headstrong Lily.

As she tried to concentrate on the passage before her titled 'Power of the Tongue' she heard the murmurs of quiet conversations below. Then she heard Frank come in and drop newly cut kindling in the wood box to start the wood stove in the morning. "Damn that Frank, he was supposed to wake me!" she thought to herself. "Just wait 'til I get a hold of that brother of mine!"

Frank, now eighteen and two years older than Lily, looked a lot like their father. About five foot nine, slender, with slightly wavy black hair and piercing dark eyes. But unlike his father's stern and even approach, he could have flashes of temper which tended to land him in trouble from time to time.

The Millett Residence had two bedrooms upstairs and one bedroom downstairs next to the kitchen for Jennie Bell and George. A large living room in the front of the building reached from one side of the house to the other. Like most homes, the kitchen was the area where everyone tended to gather. It was always warmer there in the fall and winter as the kitchen stove would always be stoked with firewood. A large pot bellied wood stove was also in the living room, but normally not used too much except in the winter or in the event that company or family came calling.

The hushed conversations below gradually ceased and Lily heard the creak of Frank's footsteps on the wooden treads as he slowly came upstairs. He was carrying a lantern and she could make out the dim light coming in under the door as he walked past to his room. "I'll deal with him tomorrow," she thought as she lay the Bible on the night stand and blew out her own lantern before snuggling down under a homemade feather quilt.

The next thing she heard was her mother's voice calling, "Lily, time to get up. Your father and Frank are out milking the cows. The table needs to be set, so hurry up. And be sure and bring your father's Bible down with you,"

Lily had slept hard. School, coupled with the evening and weekend job at Rosco's, combined to take the bulk of her energy. Groggily she sat up, stretched and began to dress.

While Frank was finishing milking their two cows, George led their dappled gray out of the barn, put on the eye blinders, horse collar and reins, then backed him up to their weather worn black buggy. After fastening the wagon tongue to the single tree he brought the carriage out to the front of the house and tied Old Tom's reins to one of the posts at the front porch.

"Hurry up. The bacon is frying," she heard again from down below.

By the time Lily got downstairs her father and brother were just coming in for breakfast. After everyone had eaten, the morning dishes were done, then the family started to prepare for church as they began changing into their Sunday best clothes.

The family filed out of the house and into the old buggy. Lily and Frank sat on a home made bench behind the seat. The buggy had no top as it had long since deteriorated in the weather so George Millett had taken the rest of the framework off. For a change, the sun was shining brightly so they did not take any umbrellas.

The First Methodist Church was located on the corner of McKinley and Harrison Street in an old house that had been donated for use by Stanley Harrison, president and owner of the New Line Bank in downtown Tacoma. The building had been repossessed by the bank, and in truth, the bank was unable to sell it because of its run down condition. The shrewd banker knew that the parish folks would have to repair the building to make it usable, and so far the members had replaced the roof and rebuilt the foundation. If their meager collections allowed they had future plans to repair and paint the rest of the building, however Mr. Harrison still retained title to the property and looked forward to a profitable sale sometime in the future.

Reverend Elias Rush was from a small town somewhere in Indiana and had come west at the urging of his older brother who had a small logging operation in Tacoma. Through his brother he had met Mr. Harrison and made the arrangement to use the old building as a meeting house for his small flock. The Reverend was a small, but determined man with a neatly trimmed black beard, although his dark head of hair was often in need of being cut. He had arrived in Tacoma in the summer of 1890 and, by persistence and a lot of persuasion, his membership had grown to nearly twenty families. Not great, but it was increasing in a place where rough hewn loggers, sailors and fortune seekers were abundant.

His sermon this morning was a slightly subdued version of a hell and brimstone speech and it made Lily uneasy. She had read and reread the scriptures that her father told her to, and mentally questioned why everyone was going to hell if they said the wrong words and did not attend this church. Other people that she knew who did not attend this church, or any other, appeared quite happy with life. Why was this weight not put on them? It did not make sense to her.

After what seemed like hours to Lily the small congregation was dismissed and began to file out of the partially refurbished building. They paused and shook hands with Reverend Rush and everyone told him what a great sermon he had preached, just the same as every other Sunday. It all seemed so boring and superficial to Lilly.

The ride home was quite relaxed and there was a light conversation was about Reverend Rush's sermon, which Lily carefully avoided. She did not want to remind her father of his lecture to her the prior evening. Other mundane topics about the beautiful day, their neighbors and their problems, as well as crops planted and the fields that still had to be cleared were discussed. All dull items to the sixteen year old girl.

As they neared the Baker home Lily asked, "Can I stop and see Anna?"

"I suppose so," replied her father as he pulled back on old Tom's reins, "but remember to come home early and help your mother with the chores."

"I will," she replied as she hopped off the buggy and began running towards the house.

She heard her mother behind add, "It's not 'can I'. It's 'may I'. And don't get that dress dirty!" she admonished. "Father, sometimes I just wonder about that girl."

Anna Baker's little twelve year old sister June, answered Lily's knock on the door, then turned and yelled out over her shoulder, "Anna, Lily's here!"

Anna and Lily had been best friends since they started the first grade together at Adams Elementary. Often as they walked to and from school they confided in each other about their deepest concerns. Because of this closeness the two of them were soon out in back of the Baker house and Lily began to voice her frustration. "My father threw a fit because mother told him I said 'damn'. Can you imagine that! Then, I had to go to my room and read the Bible!"

Anna pushed some pesky hair back away from her eye, "That's not such a bad word. I heard the Townsend boys saying a lot worse than that."

"But it's so unfair! Boys get away with it! Sometimes I want to tell everyone to go to hell!"

"Lily!"

"Oh Anna, I mean it. If it wasn't for you to talk to I don't know what I'd do. My parents are such prudes! Believe me, I hear a lot worse than that at Rosco's. The dock workers are the worst, although the loggers and construction crews really swear too. You should hear some of the things they say."

"I don't know if I want to."

"Although that good looking Ben Chandler that comes in is a real gentleman. I really like him," Lily's face brightened, "And you should see how he torments Rosco about how easy he has it, and Rosco has to take it because Ben is a such good customer."

Anna again pushed the annoying wisps of hair away from her eye. "What's this Ben like? And just how old is he?"

"Oh, he's gorgeous with wavy dark brown hair that he combs back on the sides."

"Yes, but how old is he?"

"I don't know, but he's old enough to go to the McKinley Hill dance last night. Oh, I wanted to go so bad, but even if he asked me, my folks would throw a fit."

"Well, how old do you think he is?" Anna persisted.

"Maybe twenty-one, or twenty-two. I don't know."

"Oh, wow! And he's not married?"

"Of course not, or he wouldn't be bragging about going to the dance."

"He sounds absolutely wonderful."

"Oh he is. I guess you would call him," she hesitated looking for the right word, then added, 'smooth'. But, he doesn't even know I'm alive. Oh, he kids around with me sometimes, but I just don't know how to get him to really notice me."

Anna leaned back and stared at her friend. "Perhaps if you bobbed your hair and got one of those new curling irons."

"Oh, I couldn't do that. I know my folks would throw a fit! Mother's always saying, 'you have such beautiful long dark hair'. I get so tired hearing that!"

"Another thing, you might try some of that bright red lip rouge that they now have in the stores."

"Oh Anna, that would be bizarre. I could never do that!" She looked towards the west at the setting sun. "Oh oh, it's getting late. I'd better go now. I have to help get dinner ready."

However, Anna's suggestions were not lost on the young woman and she quietly tucked the ideas away.

It seemed that spring flew by, then summer came and went, bringing the onset of vivid fall colors. The large maple trees waved their golden leaves at the autumn skies, while the shorter vine maple leaves turned into brilliant shades of reds.

Now was the time that families and neighbors chipped in to pick the fall fruit and vegetables, mow the fields and gather the hay. Firewood was cut and stacked in preparation for another approaching dreary wet and snowy winter. The economy was slow. Money was tight, but everyone was in the same situation, so no one really thought of themselves as being poor. The Millett family fared no better or worse than their neighbors. They had a small orchard on one corner of their modest twenty acres raising apples, pears, and peaches. Another area was set aside for growing vegetables. The remainder of the ground was used as grazing for their two horses and two cows. Like their neighbors, they traded back and forth. Lily's dad often swapped fruit and vegetables for firewood, or hay for his livestock. And occasionally, he would get a side job making cabinets for someone.

Lily had worked full time at Rosco's all summer, and when school began again, she returned to working evenings and Saturdays only. She had long forgotten about getting even with her brother Frank. The long days she endured, coupled with her chores at home as well as school, left her little time for anything else.

Suddenly December was upon them and it was time to prepare for the Yuletide season. Most of the presents exchanged during Christmas were home made. There were hand made clothes of various descriptions and colors, quilted blankets, embroidered or crocheted table cloths and table napkins, greeting cards, home made cabinets, as well as hand carved items.

This year Frank got to pick out and cut down the family Christmas tree. He built a stand for the tree and stood it up the living room. Colored paper chains and strings of popcorn were wound around the tree. The trim was completed with a large silver star on the top.

Christmas morning the gifts that were put under the tree the night before were exchanged. Lily received a new hand knitted scarf and a quilted blanket crisscrossed with squares of red and green flannel. It would be her 'Christmas Blanket' she announced proudly as she held it up for all to see. Frank received a new pair of much needed work boots. Jennie Bell got a promissory note for a sewing cabinet from George that he had not quite finished, and George received a small, all metal plane, that he needed to finish off the woodwork.

In the morning after the gift exchange the family bundled up and took the buggy to the church. After a special service by Reverend Rush, they hurried home to contemplate their good fortunes as provided by their creator. The rest of the day was set aside for enjoying good food and the hospitality of friends and neighbors. Jennie Bell had roasted one of their roosters for their Christmas meal, which she served with mashed potatoes, gravy, a green salad, baked yams,and mincemeat pie for dessert. George said the family blessing at the table. Overall it was a quiet and peaceful time. A time for personal thoughts and a time to look towards the future year.

Lily's seventeenth birthday on January ninth came and went with an almost an air of indifference. Her mother made a small cake, and other than the birthday cards she received from family, it was just another school day, mundane chores, and a workday at the restaurant.

The next day after school was over Anna handed Lily a small package. "I was going to give this to you this morning on the way to school, but I still had to wrap it. I took some paper from the art supply drawer. I hope you like it. It's for your birthday."

Lily quickly tore open the colorful pink and white package. Inside was a small pot of red 'Rose Petal' lip rouge. "Oh, Anna it's wonderful. Oh, thank you, thank you!" she replied dropping the small capsule in her purse, "but I've got to go now, or I'll be late for work. See you in the morning." As she turned to leave she looked back at Anna once more, and mouthed silently 'thank you'. She wondered what she would ever do if it wasn't for dear Anna.

When Lily arrived at Rosco's she immediately applied her new lip rouge, perhaps a bit too heavy, and then stepped forward to work her four hour evening shift. She felt a bit self conscious at first, but soon forgot about it as she busied herself with the evenings customers. Mostly farm laborers and transient loggers who had come in for a inexpensive warm meal and a cup of coffee before looking for a room to spend the night.

At the end of the shift Lily counted up her tips and realized she had accumulated twenty-three cents in her tip cup. It was more than double that of any other day, including Saturdays when business was best. She tried to think what had made the difference. It had to be how she looked, she decided, and it had to be the lip rouge. It must have made her look older and more mature. She thought, "Perhaps if I were to bob my hair and have it curled like Anna suggested I might do even better."

She had been saving her tips during the summer months and now she realized she could afford the one dollar and fifty cents to go to Francene's Hair Emporium down on Pacific Avenue for a bob and a treatment with a curling iron. It was so very tempting.

As she stood with a small mirror in her hand, she studied the image that stared back at her. Carefully she wiped the telltale color from her lips before she left Rosco's. No need to upset her mother and father with her "new look". She knew that they would not understand that she was no longer a child, but rather a young woman wanting more out of life than a boring, stale and stuffy farm life existence. Let her brother Frank have that, but it would not be the life for her.

Eventually Lily began to make plans to get her hair bobbed, regardless of how her family might feel about it. She got Rosco to give her next Friday evening off, and made an a four thirty appointment at Francene's Hair Emporium.

Later in the week while walking to school with Anna Baker, she told her of her plans. "I'm going to go ahead and get my hair completely changed this Friday, just like you suggested. I've saved my tip money up, and I've already made an appointment with Francene's downtown. I know that my parents will throw a fit, but I'm going to do it anyway. Now, I need your help. Can I stay at your house on Friday night?"

"Of course, my folks won't mind, but what will that solve? You'll still have to go out on Saturday."

"I know. I'll leave your house on Saturday morning and go straight to work like normal, then I'll go to my house that evening. I'll keep my head covered and go right up to my room. I'll tell my parents that I don't feel well and want to go right to bed. Father will see my hair bob on Sunday morning, and….."

"And what will he do?" asked Anna.

"Oh, since it's Sunday, he'll probably say I'm going to hell and will have me reading the Bible again, possibly memorizing some passages that I'll have to recite back to him. Then he'll probably have me confess all my horrible sinful ways to Reverend Rush."

"I guess that doesn't sound too bad."

The week moved slowly for Lily, but she was determined to go through with her plan. When Friday finally came she went directly to Francene's Hair Emporium after school. First, she had a quick wash out. As her hair was being combed out, Francene asked, "Are you sure that you want it bobbed? That's pretty short you realize."

"Yes, I'm sure."

Lily began watching as her long auburn tresses were cut and fell silently to the floor. Francene worked her scissors and comb continually as she snipped and cut around her neck and ears. After towel drying she used a hot curling iron with a setting solution to style her new look.

Lily was mesmerized as she watched the transformation take place in the mirror. A beautiful young woman with curly short hair barely below her ears began to appear. Skillfully and subtly Francene combed the sides back so it would appear to look that way naturally.

"Now my dear," Francene commented, "let's add a touch of blush to your cheek. This rainy climate can leave a lady's skin too ashen, and also we'll add a bit color to your brow. Not too much, just a hint. Got to show the boys what beauties we ladies really are, even if it does take a little extra touch here and there."

"I absolutely love it!" Lily gushed. "It looks so, so wonderful!"

"The only other thing is the proper hat for you. Something small, not too pretentious, perhaps with a small bow in it. You'll have to look around for just the right thing. Why not try Johnson's Millinery up on St. Helens Avenue. I'm sure he will have just the right one to set off your new look."

"Oh, thank you. I will," replied Lily as she turned around and around to admire her new appearance in the mirror, then reached for her purse by her long dark coat on the chair and carefully counted out Francene's fee. After leaving the hair salon she caught the hay burner special, getting off at Jake's Corner and proceeded to the Baker's residence. Anna's sister, June answered her knock at the door.

"Oh Lily, you look so different," she said as she stared wide eyed, before finally turning and yelling towards the kitchen in the back of the house, "Anna, Lily's here."

Presently Anna came out of the kitchen with a dish towel still in her hand. "Well, don't just stand there June. Let her in."

Obediently, but still in awe, June stepped out of the way.

As Anna came up behind her little sister, she took off her apron and threw it and the damp dish towel over June's shoulder. "Here, take these to the kitchen," she ordered.

"Lily, you got here sooner than I expected. Come on in. Let's go up to my room. Oh, you look fabulous."

"Do you really think so? I know I really like it," Lily said as they entered Anna's bedroom, shutting the door behind them. "You're not just saying that?"

"No, no. I think it makes you look like a sophisticated woman. Oh, the boys will certainly notice you now."

The rest of the evening they spent in Anna's room talking about Lily's new appearance. Every little detail was studied and debated. They discussed the application of the makeup including blush and lip rouge, and the possible purchase of a hat like Francene had recommended, until the two were worn out and finally went to bed. After all, Lily still had to work tomorrow, then she had to go home and face her father on the following Sunday morning.

She arrived at Rosco's early on Saturday morning and before Rosco noticed her, she took a small mirror from under the counter and careful applied her treasured lip rouge. Not quite as heavy as before as Francene had mentioned that just a touch was always the best way to go. Finally satisfied with her appearance, she replaced the mirror and taking her apron off the wooden wall peg began to tie it on just as Rosco walked out of the kitchen.

"I Thought I heard someone come in. My God girl, I almost didn't recognize you with that short hair. Why you look all growed up and all!"

Lily acknowledged Rosco's comments with an extra blush to her cheeks, then moved over by the large coffee pot at the end of the stove. "I've got to get the coffee ready and set a place for Mr. Tendick. He'll be here any minute," she said trying to change the subject, but inwardly she was very pleased by his remarks.

"Yeah, right. Let's get things going around here. I can't afford to stand here gabbing all day," Rosco replied as he turned and walked back into his kitchen.

The day started out just like most of all the others at the small cafe. Some new customers from the Northern Pacific Railroad came in. Then the usual morning regulars came by, ordering the same thing daily, with of course a few exceptions. During the morning Lily heard some complimentary remarks by some of the regulars about her new look and silently beamed from within. Her tip cup also had a few more coins than normal.

The morning quickly passed and soon they were cleaning and preparing for the lunch crowd. The day was going very well and Lily began to feel more and more confident with her new look. She was feeling more relaxed and happy as she started to joke and talk more freely with the customers while she worked.

At three thirty Lily had just finished cleaning up from the noon rush as Ben Chandler came in. He walked up to the counter and sat down on a stool at the end of the bar. "Give me a cup of coffee and one of Rosco's special rolls." Then he glanced at Lily again, "Well, I'll be! Lily, I almost didn't recognize you! Why you look like a little Greek goddess!"

As she turned to get one of Rosco's rolls from out of the cabinet a blush of red tinted her neck and ears. It was music to her ears. Ben had finally taken notice and she was thrilled almost beyond words. She turned and handed him a small plate with one of the rolls. "I'll, I'll get your coffee," she stammered as she took a cup from the coffee rack and poured the coffee. She set the cup in front of Ben, then remembered to grab the sugar and a spoon for him.

At that moment she heard the restaurant door open violently and her father's loud booming voice yell, "Lily! Get your coat! You're coming home right now!"

George Millett continued across the room, stepped behind counter and grabbed Lily's arm. "Paul Baker told me of your blasphemy. I said grab your coat! We're leaving this den of iniquity!"

Upon hearing the uproar Rosco rushed out of the kitchen, "What the hell's going on out here?" He pulled up short as he saw it was Lily's father, then asked "George, what the hell's the matter? What's going on? You can't just bust in here and start a ruckus like this."

Lily began to cry as her father continued his tirade. "I can, and I will," he yelled violently at Rosco. "I never wanted Lily to come to work here in the first place, in this, this hole of Satan! And I was right! Look how you have corrupted my daughter!" He turned back to Lily, "I said get your coat! You are going home right now!"

Ben Chandler stood up and made a feeble attempt to assist, "Really, she's just fine, we've all......

"Quiet! Just keep your nose out of things that don't concern you!" said George as he turned and glared at the interloper.

Lily scooped up her coat and purse with her free hand as her father pulled her towards the door just as two men were coming in. "Get out of the way!" George yelled at the startled customers as he pushed Lily out the doorway. "Get up there on that buggy right now!"

One of the customers looked back out the door and asked, "What was that all about?"

"Nothing to be concerned about. Come on in. What can I get you boys? Coffee? You name it," said Rosco as he tried to quickly smooth over the event. He wanted it to be business as usual.

It definitely was not business as usual for Lily. During the ride home she sat on the lightly padded buggy seat softly crying. How could her father have done such a thing. It was degrading.

Not one word was said on the ride home. Frank was walking towards the barn when they arrived home and George yelled to him, "Frank, take Old Tom here and put him in the barn. Water him down and feed him, and be sure to put the buggy in the lean-to."

Frank ran up to do his father's bidding, then he stood with his mouth open as he recognized Lily beside him.

"Don't just stand there! Grab the reins and do what I said!'

"Yes father," he replied as he reached out for the lines.

"Lily, into the house right now!"

As Lily stepped down from the buggy her mother came out of the back door of the house. "What is happening? Oh heaven's to be! Oh my! Heaven's to be! Lily child, what have you done with yourself?"

"Jennie Bell, your daughter has seen the ways of the Devil himself! I warned you that this would happen, but you wouldn't listen!" He took Lily by the arm, "Into the house young lady!"

Once inside, Lily was made to sit at the kitchen table as her father continued his harangue. "We are going to get this over with right here and now! Don't you realize that cutting your hair like that makes you a servant of the Devil?"

"But, father...."

"But, father nothing! All painted up like that, you look like a harlot!"

"George, it's really not that bad," said Jennie Bell as she tried to calm her husband down.

On the ride home Lily knew roughly what was coming and had been slowly trying to compose herself for the ordeal. She made up her mind that she had a right to dress the way she wanted to, and although she knew they would be very upset, she didn't realize that her father would be so incensed. She had miscalculated his reaction and now tried to reason with him. "Father, I haven't changed. I'm still the same person."

"You've become beholden to the very Devil himself! A real hussy!"

Jenny Bell tried again to intercede, "Really George, I...."

George turned to his wife, "It's true. Look at her! Her hair! That lip coloring!" He looked back at Lily. "Then, I found out from Mr. Baker that you did this yesterday and you tried to hide it from us! That makes you a liar and a cheat in the eyes of the Lord!"

Lily stood up defiantly, "I am a grown adult. I am not changing my look back to the same old nothingness that I was, and you have no right to ask me to. I'll move out if I have to!"

"I have every right in the world, and as long as you live under my roof, you will obey the rules of the Lord and the rules of this household. If you go out of our doorway, you will never be welcome in this house again! You will cease to exist!"

"Then father, you leave me no choice. I'm leaving!"

Her mother began crying, "George, you can not do this. She is our only daughter," she wailed.

"Jennie Bell, she has made her own pact with the Devil. Let her go with him."

Lily reached out for her coat, picked up her purse and walked out the back door. It would be the last time she would ever see her parents, her brother or her home.

She walked aimlessly down the road, trying to calm down, trying ease her fears, trying to stop her tears and trying to think of where to go and what to do next. Dusk was starting and the sun was dropping below the tree line in the west. She saw Anna's Baker's house and decided to ask if she could spend the night. She mustered up her courage and walked up to the front door and knocked quietly.

After what seemed an eternity, Anna's mother, Cleo, opened the door. "Lily, do come in. Oh, you've been crying. Please come inside. What seems to be the problem?"

Anna and June heard her mother answer the door and both came to see who was calling.

"Come in child. Sit down and tell us what has happened," Cleo said as she led Lily over by the table and pulled out a chair for her to sit on.

In between gasping sobs, and through a steady stream of tears, Lily slowly began to tell them what had taken place. Then Anna and her mother related that Lily's dad had come over to see about a plow. Paul Baker casually mentioned that Lily had gotten a haircut and had stayed overnight. Upon hearing about that, George Millet suddenly became very quiet and left abruptly. From there he evidently went directly to Rosco's and pulled Lily out of the small restaurant.

Gradually everyone regained their composure and the Bakers' insisted that Lily stay with them until things returned somewhat to normal and the future could then be decided.

Lily stayed at the Baker's home the next day and did not go to church, nor did she go to school on the following Monday. Instead she decided to go down to Rosco's and ask for her job back. The Bakers' said she could stay with them until she was able to support herself. However, when she approached Rosco Howell, he told her that he had already hired a replacement and that he had no other openings. He did pay her three dollars for the prior weeks work, and as he was counting out the money, Lily looked at her tip cup under the counter. It was empty.

She was very depressed upon leaving the small restaurant. She now had a grand total of four dollars and forty-two cents in her purse. It was very demoralizing. She knew she had to find work soon as the Bakers could not afford to feed and board her for very long. She discussed the problem with the Bakers and tried to assure them she would not be a burden, and that she would pay them back for their kindness and hospitality.

That's when Anna remembered a cousin of theirs who owned a restaurant in Seattle. "Let's write to P.J. Maybe he has an opening."

The Baker's cousin, was P.J. Concannon, an ex-city detective who owned and operated an upscale restaurant called The Rochester House on Pike Street along the waterfront in Seattle.

Quickly they sat down and composed a letter extolling the virtues of Lily's restaurant experience and briefly outlining the difficult situation that she was in. The next day Lily posted the letter and silently crossed her fingers while wishing for a speedy reply.

School was over for her now. She had to support herself and she was very determined that she would not beg to go back home. The days passed slowly as

Lily continued to knock on doors looking for work in the Tacoma area, all to no avail.

On April nineteenth a letter from P.J. Concannon arrived addressed to Miss Lily Millett, in care of the Baker family. Everyone eagerly gathered around as Lily nervously tore open the letter and started to read. Then Lily yelled, "I've got a job, I've got a job!"

They all took turns reading the letter. Not only did she have a job, but P.J. had friends who would rent her a room near the restaurant for three dollars a week. Plus all her meals would be free at the restaurant! A very happy and much relieved Lily Millet went to sleep that night.

Early the following morning as Anna was leaving for school, Lily hugged and kissed her dear friend goodbye, then turned and gave little June a hug as she followed her older sister out the door. Next Lily gathered up her few belongings and said a tearful goodbye to Cleo Baker before leaving to catch the ten o'clock morning train to Seattle.

Upon arriving in Seattle, she asked directions to Pike Street and began her search for the Rochester House restaurant which she located only about six blocks from the railroad station. It was a large cream colored building facing out towards the piers on the waterfront. She hesitated briefly, took a big deep breath and entered the imposing structure. "I'm looking for Mr. P.J. Concannon," she said to the immaculately groomed young man behind the counter.

He looked up, gave a superficial smile, and pointed towards the back of the room. "He's in his office at the far end of the hall, past the dining room."

"Thank you," replied Lily as she turned and walked along the side of the large dinning room filled with customers who were seated at tables covered with white table cloths, vases with fresh roses, and elegant table ware. At the end of the hall was a sign on a dark wooden door which read, "P.J. Concannon, Proprietor". She knocked quietly.

"Come in," said the booming voice from inside.

Lily opened the door and entered the large office, trying not to be intimidated by the opulent surroundings she was seeing. She forced herself to speak up confidently, "I'm Lily Millett. You wrote me a letter. Actually you wrote the letter to me in care of the Bakers' in Tacoma."

A tall man in a white shirt and black bow tie stood up from behind a large mahogany desk. "Ah yes, Miss Lily Millett. I got your inquiry and also your recommendations from my cousins. May I call you Lily?"

"Yes sir"

"Good. Now then Lily, how are my cousins doing?" he asked as he stroked at his large drooping mustache. "Please be seated."

"They're doing just fine sir, and they send their regards," she answered as she began to appraise this tall and impressive man. He stood about six foot four inches, just slightly over weight. The very picture she decided of an ex-policeman.

"No need to call me 'sir'. I'm just known as 'P.J.' to all my employees. Now, let's see. You got here a little quicker than I thought, but I've already talked to my friends, Lorraine and Jack Palmer." He paused to sit down, then scribbled out an address on a piece of paper. "Here, take this. It's only about three blocks due north of here. They have a boarding house called Palmer Arms and they'll put you up." He reached across his desk and handed Lily the paper. "Now then, can you come in at nine in the morning?"

"Yes sir. I mean, yes P.J."

"Good. Russell at the front desk will let you in. See Angelina, and she'll start teaching you the ropes here. Oh, have you eaten?"

"Yes," she fibbed, then bit her lip realizing she could probably have had a free meal. However, she still had three dollars and sixty-seven cents in her purse. Enough to pay for her room for a week and little left over for a few modest meals, not counting the free food that she would be getting from her new employer.

An extremely elated Lily left P.J.'s office. It had worked out! She had a job, and not only that, she was out on her own in this big, wide wonderful world! And P.J. seemed very nice. "I won't let him down", she silently promised herself.

The weather in western Washington and the Puget Sound area can be very dismal at times, especially in the winter season when it seems to rain almost everyday. The year of Eighteen Ninety-four proved no exception to the rule. In spite of the rain, mist, fog and often an accompanying bone numbing chill, Lily enjoyed the Seattle waterfront with its views of cargo ships coming and going. It was an exciting place to be and she was in the middle of it all where she could see the building of a new and challenging city.

There were the Chinese who worked at many of the menial shipping jobs and had their own community nearby. A large portion of the city's elite had homes up on Queen Anne Hill over looking the business district. People were also building luxury homes way out on Magnolia Bluff and up on Beacon Hill. Many Scandinavians who worked in the logging industry lived further north in a district called Ballard. Even a part of the western peninsula known as West Seattle was beginning to flourish. It had truly become an exotic place, earning the nickname of 'The Emerald City'.

Lily loved the excitement of it all. She had a great job, a wonderful boss and she had began to save a little money as well. What could be better! She even sent a money order to the Bakers' in Tacoma to help pay them for the kindness that they had extended. Additionally she continued to maintain a correspondence with her best friend Anna. Deciding that everything was far too exciting to not keep a record of, she bought a diary and began recording everyday events in it. She started from the time she had left home up to the present and continued to make an entry almost everyday.

She began to blossom into a very pretty young lady and had even managed to buy the small hat with a little white bow on the top like the one that Francene in Tacoma had recommended. Her wardrobe grew slowly as she carefully shopped the stores for the current fashions and the best buys.

In a very short time she became one of P.J.'s top waitress's and many of the guests dining at the Rochester House frequently asked for her by name. As a result her tips now made up about one third of her weekly salary.

Single young men suddenly began to take an interest in this pert and vivacious young woman and she soon found she could get most of them to do her bidding with a coy smile and a flirtatious wink. One of these swains was Ron Appleton, who claimed to have family ties to the Foss Tug Company, but Lily soon realized that if he had any connections, it might be as a second or third cousin only. Nevertheless, he always seemed to have money to spend. Occasionally they were seen together at plays or touring by horse and buggy on the weekends when weather permitted.

John Artibus, a tailor who owned a shop off second street, often asked her out as well. So far they had had two dates, but she found him much too stifling, too dry and too sedate. She enjoyed her freedom, and like a young eaglet, was ready to fly and sample life.

Ron, however, was gallant and exciting. One evening after a ride up on Beacon Hill, he held her hand in his and gave her his patented speech. "I love the way your eyes shine in the evening light, and how it highlights your hair, adding to your beauty."

Lily had been told by Angelina and others at work that Ron Appleton was a casanova, but his words were intoxicating. He moved closer to her, put his arm around her shoulder and kissed her softly on the lips, than again more passionately. It took her breath away and although it left her silently yearning for more she was able to politely evade his further advances. "No, not here, not now," she said modestly. "I really must go now. My landlords, Lorraine and Jack, remember you met them, are expecting me for dinner."

"At seven o'clock!" Ron questioned looking at his gold encased pocket watch.

"I know, but Sunday evening is their only free time in the week and they asked me to share it with them, and it's the only time I have free as well," replied Lily knowing her little white lie was far too obvious. She'd have to develop better and more plausible excuses for the future she quickly decided.

Ron knew that the game was over for the evening. There would be plenty of other times and he was sure he could win the young girl over to his point of view, and after all, he had not lost yet. It was merely a postponement of more exciting things to come he thought to himself as he returned to Palmer Arms and dropped Lilly off at the boarding house.

She breathed a quiet, but aroused, sigh of relief as she walked inside the building and up the stairs to her room on the second floor. She was learning how to keep a man interested, yet careful not to promise too much, and this new knowledge exhilarated her.

The summer months flew by, then fall arrived with December bringing an early snowfall of about two inches providing a wonderful white blanket over the city. However, this was immediately followed by a typical northwest light rainstorm which quickly washed away the magic. It did remind everyone though that Christmas was just around the corner and Lily tried to get into the holiday spirit. Yet without her family in Tacoma, things were not the same. Still she was determined not to be discouraged as she bought small gifts for her new friends. A silver money clip for Ron, new embroidered hankies for Angelina at work, a scarf for Russell at the front desk, and a new pen and ink set for P.J.'s desk. She bought a small oriental doll from Chinatown and mailed it to Anna along with a card for her and her family. Next she found a nicely decorated card and sent it to her estranged family.

Later, when George Millett picked up the mail from the post office in Tacoma and saw the card was from Lily, he threw it away unread.

Lilly and the rest of the staff at the Rochester House were kept busy putting up Christmas decorations. They strung them along the walls and on the small fir tree that Russell had put up in one corners. During this festive time of the year business continued to be brisk with large and small Christmas parties for their clientele.

Foss Tug Company had a large party for their executives and their families, but Lily noticed that Ron Appleton was conspicuous in his absence. Later, when they went for a walk down Pike Street, he would explain that he was meeting with a client and couldn't get away. His own little white lie Lily decided. More than likely the client was a blond that Angelina said she had seen him with earlier that day. But Ron did have a certain flair. He treated her with dignity and respect, something she had not had in the past. In spite of Angelina's subtle hints and warnings, she began to see more and more of him.

As they toured around the city Ron began to tell his acquaintances that "Lily is my girl". Unconsciously she began to accept it as well, even though she was slightly uncomfortable with the label. She wasn't really sure she wanted to be anybody's girl yet. She was still discovering that there was much more out in the world to see and do.

Ron continued to make stronger demands on her. His kisses no longer had that tingle of romance, they were wooden and hard. His hands no longer caressed her curves, but now became probing arms that tried to constantly undo her clothing. Her resistance built as he became more demanding. "Ron, no," she said one evening at the door outside her small room. "You can't come in. Let go of my arm!"

He squeezed her arm tightly and said, "Look here Lily, you are mine! I own you! You will do anything I want, and I want you now!"

With her free right arm she reached back and slapped his face as hard as she could, "I don't care want you want! You leave right now or I'll yell for help. I swear I will scream for help!"

Slowly Ron released the grip on her arm. His eyes glared with anger as he said, "You are my girl and no one else's. Don't you ever forget it!" His jaw was tightly clenched as he scowled at her. "Don't you even think about going out with another man because I will find you. You are mine. Mine only! Do you understand that?"

Lily stood scared and trembling as she nodded yes, then said very quiet and meekly, "I have to go in now." She turned her back on him, not knowing if he would attack her or not. She opened the door and walked into her room while he continued to watch and glower at her as she shut the door in his face.

Lily stood by the door until she heard his footsteps walk away and go down the stairwell, then quietly locked the door, walked over to her bed and sat down to try regain her composure. It had been a very frightening experience. She had never been though anything like that before. She had seen the anger and rage with her refusal and she worried about what he really might be capable of. Finally, she rose and got ready for bed, determined to avoid Mister Ron Appleton in the future.

Earlier, three weeks before Christmas, P.J. announced that on the twenty-fourth they would not be open for regular business. At that point he invited all of his employees to a Christmas party at the restaurant which would start at noon and end at approximately three to four o'clock the same day. All together there were fifteen employees counting the two cooks in the kitchen, two dish washers, eight waitresses, Russell from the front desk, P.J.'s bookkeeper, and P.J. himself.

P.J. was generous to all. He had drinks set out for everyone to go with their main course dinner of fresh salmon, steak, or fried chicken. This was followed with tasty and fancy varieties of cakes and pies for dessert. During the meal he complimented his entire staff for a job well done, then passed out pay envelopes with Christmas bonus checks inside. Lily was thrilled to open hers later and find a check for ten dollars. She didn't know what the other employees had received, but she was extremely happy to receive such a large bonus.

The Rochester House moved into a short period of New Years Eve parties that were held on the twenty-ninth, thirtieth and thirty-first. She was grateful for the increase in work hours because she could then use her job as an excuse for not going out with Ron Appleton.

The parties were private, and somewhat boisterous, but Lily enjoyed them all, even though the work was long and the customers could be demanding. A few of the party attendees always got a bit tipsy, but as a general rule everything was all in good fun, and the best part was that these parties usually tipped very well. However, P.J. insisted that all tips be divided up among all of his help contrary to most other restaurant policies in Seattle. Lily thought it was the fair thing to do, as no one could do a good job without the kitchen help. She didn't know exactly how the tips were divided, but she was very happy with the results. Results that now often equaled half of her normal salary.

The first week of January brought a heavy snow storm to the city. Almost twelve inches fell on the foothills of Seattle which severely limited business and all the transportation in the city. Some businesses closed for three to four days as the hills became layered in ice and were too slippery for people, horses and wagons to get around. Then it warmed up again bringing rain which soon brought and end to the packed snow and ice, but brought with it another problem. One of muddy streets and thoroughfares. The business owners complained vehemently to city officials about the poor road conditions. The situation was so bad that many owners went out on their own to haul in gravel from the nearby quarries to try and ease the problem.

Even business at the Rochester House had tapered off due to the horrible weather, but they still managed to retain most of their regular clientele. P.J. allowed anyone who wanted time off during this slow period to take it, but only two of the staff took advantage of it, as there was really nothing else to do unless one took a trip, and traveling was certainly limited by the weather.

Ron Appleton continued to pressure Lily for dates in his endeavor to to win her over. But Lily had learned a variety of excuses. Like, "I have to work early in the morning, too much wine gives me a headache, I promised the Jones's that I'd drop by this evening at eight, I have laundry to take care of, and so on. As a result, she spent the evening of her eighteenth birthday on January ninth with her new friend Angelina. She purposely did not mention her birthday to Ron Appleton because she knew he would use it as an excuse to try and get her to drink more and lose her inhibitions. Lily was very determined not to become one of his conquests.

Spring doesn't bring too much of a change to the northwest. Things warm up to be sure, but the rains still hang on, just not quite as heavy as during the winter months. The sun shines off and on, bringing life anew to the alder, maple and fruit trees as they start to green out and begin to match the deep green of the surrounding statuesque Douglas Fir trees.

April was typical as it continued with light showers and Lily was glad she only had to tolerate the rain for about three blocks on her way to and from work. It was nice to work indoors where it was dry and get to see and meet many of Seattle's aristocracy.

On Tuesday, the eighth, she was busy serving Mister and Mrs. Dodge crab cocktails at noontime when she heard a familiar voice call out, "Lily, Lily, is that you?"

She turned at the sound of the voice. It was Ben Chandler with another gentleman! "Uh, yes. Hello Ben," she managed to say with her heart in her mouth. "I'll be with you in a moment. You and your friend can sit right up front by the window," she added as she noticed the older gray haired and slightly balding man accompanying Ben.

Lily tried to show no extra emotion while she served Ben and his friend that he introduced as Vernon Tibbs. Inwardly she was a quiver with a sensation of anticipation. Her good looking and handsome Ben! He hadn't changed one bit. His curly brown hair was still combed beautifully back on the sides, but he now had a thin brown mustache which seemed to accent and improve his appearance even more than she remembered.

Ben and Mister Tibbs slowly ate their business man's special lunch consisting of a small salmon steak, served with a salad and a large bowl of creamed tomato soup. As Lily waited on their table, and other tables in her corner of the large dinning room, she noticed that the two men were busy in a quiet conversation and writing down notes and figures in small notebooks.

After finishing their meal the two men rose, shook hands as if agreeing on something, then proceeded towards Russell at the front counter. As Ben walked by Lily, he paused and said, "It's great to see you again."

"Same here. You look great," she said with her heart a flutter.

"Say, what time do you get off? Maybe we could get together for coffee or something?"

"Oh, that would be great. I get off at six tonight," she said hastily. "Wonderful. I'll meet you here at that time, if that would be okay?"

"Fine Ben. I'd like that."

The rest of the work day went extremely slow for Lily. Just the thought of him excited her and she could hardly wait until quitting time. In preparation she asked Angelina to cover the last few customers at her station so she would be able meet Ben promptly at six. Now, they could be together at last!

At six, Ben came through the door and saw Lily waiting at the front desk. "Hi, Lily. I've got a horse and a covered buggy outside. I borrowed it from Vernon Tibbs. I don't like walking in the rain if we don't have to."

Lily retrieved her coat and purse from the coat room behind Russell's front desk. "Okay, I'm ready to go."

"Let me help you with your coat," said Ben as he reached out and helped her put it on.

"Thank you," was her hushed reply as they both turned and walked out the door.

He helped her up into the buggy, then walked around to get into the seat beside her. It was a cloudy evening, but it was not raining at the moment and for that Lily was grateful.

"I saw a little place down by the fish market that looks interesting. We could stop in there for a cup of tea, or perhaps coffee if you like," said Ben as he picked up the reins to the old brown horse in front and gave a gentle slap on the horse's back.

"That would be just fine."

The clop, clop of the horse's hooves, mingled with the noise of the iron rims on the buggy wheels hitting against the cobbles. The sound echoed in the evening air and it made it difficult to hold a good conversation. Fortunately it was not far to the Harbor Cafe which proved to be a clean establishment that was brightly lit by hanging kerosene lanterns.

Once inside, they chose a small booth along one of the side walls. Ben ordered coffee and a cinnamon roll, which Lily recalled was one of his favorite things when he used to come into Rosco's place in Tacoma. "I'll just have coffee only," she said to the aproned middle aged man who came to serve them.

"Well Lily, tell me how you've been. I haven't seen you since that day your father dragged you out of Rosco's. What have you been up to?"

Lily patiently explained to Ben how she had left home after that incident, had been befriended by the Baker family, and how she ended up working for P.J. in Seattle. "And how about you? What have you been doing, and how did you know I was at the Rochester House?"

"Actually I didn't. It was just by chance that I came in there. I had a business meeting with Vernon Tibbs. He's in the produce business and lives up here in Seattle."

"And what are you and Mr. Tibbs plotting?"

Ben took a sip of the steaming hot coffee, "Actually we're just completing a business deal."

"Oh, what type may I ask?"

"We are going into business together."

"But, I thought you had a job with that freight company in Tacoma."

"I do, or rather I did." He took a bite out of the cinnamon roll and continued, "That was just a job. Now, I have the chance to own part of a freight business. Mr. Tibbs and I are going to start up our own business between Tacoma and Seattle."

Lily sat back, anxious to hear the whole exciting story.

"We've decided to call it 'C and T Hauling', and we'll haul freight from the new railroad companies that are coming into Tacoma up here to Seattle. Since Tibbs is in the produce business, we'll haul his produce back to Tacoma. The way we see it is that with the bulk of the railroad business now in Tacoma, we'll have a ready made market for our service with the railroad companies and the boating industry. And don't forget, there are a lot of freight boats coming into Tacoma also. Plus, I'm sure I can get contracts down there and he already has contracts up here in Seattle."

"Oh Ben, how wonderful! How soon will all this happen? Will you be coming to Seattle often? Will you be moving up here?" she asked hopefully.

He sat back, "Wait, wait. One question at a time. We have to get the business papers made up; Vernon Tibbs is handling that. I have to line up some help, find wagons and horses to buy. It all takes time."

"Oh goodness. How will you pay for all of that?"

"That's the good part. Tibbs is putting up the money, and he feels my knowledge of the business will make it a winner. I think he's right, at least I'm going to give it a try."

"Oh, that's just great!"

Ben paused to wipe some of the residue of the cinnamon roll off his chin, then changed the subject. "Lily, it's so good to see you again. You look lovely, all grown up and all."

Only slightly embarrassed, she lowered her eyes, "Why, thank you Ben." Oh, this is wonderful she thought to herself, her handsome Ben had returned and had finally taken notice of her. It was all so new and exciting!

Ben pulled out his pocket watch from his vest pocket and realized they had been talking for over two hours. "Say, I've got to get you home. I suppose you have to work tomorrow."

"Yes, I do."

As they got up from the small booth Ben helped drape her long coat over her shoulders, then paid the bill and left a tip on the table. After a short buggy ride again, he stopped in front of the Palmer Arms boarding house.

They both exchange warm looks. Finally Lily said, "Good night, and thank you for a most interesting evening."

He paused with his hands still on the reins, "Lily, when can I see you again?"

She hesitated only slightly, "Sunday is the only full day I have off."

"Great!" said Ben. "Let's go for a buggy ride on Sunday. I'll still be up this way then, so I could pick you up say around, one o'clock? Would that be okay?"

"Fine Ben, I'd like that."

Lily fairly flew up to her room on the second floor, her feet barely touching the steps. Oh, it was so wonderful! Her Ben was back! She sat down on the only chair in the sparse room, took her shoes off, and put her feet on the bed and leaned back. It had been an absolutely glorious day! She reached out for her diary and began to write. I just have to write to Anna too and share this marvelous news, she reminded herself.

The rest of the days of the week were beautiful for Lily as well. Not even the scattered showers of the season could not dampen her spirits.

"I don't know what makes you hum all the time when you're working, but I'll just bet it's not Ron Appleton!" said Angelina at work.

"And you are so right!" smiled Lily knowingly.

"And just who is this fabulous creature that has you so captivated? Is it the man who picked you up here last Monday, or was it Tuesday, after work?"

"It was Tuesday, and his name is Ben Chandler. I knew, or rather met, him when I worked in Tacoma."

"Well, just be careful my dear, because sometimes things are not always what they seem," warned Angelina.

"I will, but thanks for caring," said Lily, and with a slight hum in her voice she turned and went over to a table to check on one of her customers.

On Sunday morning Lily dressed up in her finest clothes. A white high necked blouse under an inexpensive, but sharp looking, dark blue jacket and matching skirt. The entire ensemble was topped off with her small hat with the white bow on top. To dress the hat off further, she added a small peacock feather which she had obtained from a clothing store on First Avenue. She had it tucked in the hat at a jaunty angle.

It was evident that Ben had gone out of his way to make an impression on Lily too. His dark brown shoes were highly polished and his brown suit had been carefully pressed with fresh creases. He was wearing a white shirt with about a one inch high collar. The collar was slightly opened in the front and the opening was partially covered by a large knot from his light brown ascot.

Promptly at one o'clock Ben picked Lily up at Palmer Arms and as Lily approached the buggy she noticed that he had just been to a barber shop because his hair had just been trimmed and cut, but it still retained that smooth, handsome look when combed gently back along the sides. He was just divine, she decided.

He helped her into the buggy he had borrowed again from Vernon Tibbs. "Miss Lily, you look very pretty today."

"Why thank you, Ben."

"Say, it's clear and not raining. It looks like it's going to be a pretty day. What do you say we take a ride out towards Magnolia Bluff, along Elliot Road? I understand that new road is in pretty good shape."

"That would be nice. I've never been out that way before," Lily answered.

They proceeded through the north end of Seattle and Ben turned onto the new road that George Elliot had persuaded the city to construct. "I'm a little surprised that Elliot pushed for this road because there's not that many homes out along here. I understand there are a few large expensive homes out near the end of the bluff, but that's about it."

"Well, Seattle is growing," said Lily in return. "Perhaps someday, there will be homes all along this way. Already there are lots of new places up on Queen Anne Hill. We'll see some of them when we pass by."

Elliot Way, as some of the locals were starting to call the road, was not finished at the far end, but it had been recently graded and was in good condition at the present, although it was evident that the harsh winter had caused some damage to the road base that had just been constructed the year before.

Ben followed the road to the end of the peninsula, then picked his way up an older narrow wagon road to the top of the bluff. There, he found a small unfenced field that he pulled into. "Let me tie the horse up to a tree and we can get out and enjoy the view."

"Oh Ben, the view is great up here, but the wind is a bit strong," said Lily as she remained in the buggy holding onto her hat.

"Lily, you're right. It is a bit breezy. I'll turn this thing around and we'll try to get out of this north wind."

Ben turned the horse and buggy around and they headed back down the narrow road to the bottom of the cliff. Once down off the hill top, they were in the lee of the tall timbered bluff and the wind was practically nonexistent. They followed the rough roadway back to the graded portion of Elliot Road. Ben soon found a wide area among some Madrona trees with a view of the Puget Sound and drove the horse and buggy out onto the viewpoint. After tying the reins to the front of the buggy he bent down and reached under the seat and pulled out a picnic basket. "Surprise! I was hoping that we could enjoy this from up on top of the bluff, but this place will have to do."

"Well Ben, I do declare, you are full of surprises! What have you got in there?" Lily asked eagerly.

"Just some sandwiches I had made up for the occasion, and a small bottle of wine. Nothing fancy, but I thought you might enjoy it."

"How thoughtful," she remarked, though she was a bit concerned over the wine, but tried not to show it.

Ben opened the picnic basket to find four ham and cheese sandwiches, two water glasses, and two faded white linen napkins. Ben laughed, "Evidently the Harbor Cafe does not have much of a choice in sandwiches."

"It will be just fine. I'll have one with ham only, and one with ham and cheese," she said with a smile, trying to set Ben at ease.

"One ham only coming up," Ben replied as he raised one of the slices of bread, pulled out the cheese and tossed it over the bank, then handed the sandwich to Lily. Next he took the two water glasses out of the basket and filled each one to the top with the red wine. "Here you are my dear."

"Thank you very much kind sir." Then they both laughed aloud at the situation. "Mister Chandler, might I suggest you use a different caterer next time. You know, this one does leave something to be desired," Lily said grinning from ear to ear.

They sipped the wine. "Nor does the caterer have any taste in wines. This stuff is bitter!" laughed Ben. "I guess I'll have to change suppliers for both the food and the wine in the future."

No alcohol was allowed at Lily's home in Tacoma, and she had only tasted a few of the drinks served at the Rochester House, still she followed Ben's lead, "Oh yes, certainly not a very good quality," she added knowingly.

They spent the rest of the afternoon leisurely riding in the buggy back towards the city, making a small detour along the edge of Queen Anne Hill to admire the fancy homes owned by some of Seattle's elite.

"Someday, I'd like to have a fancy home like one of those with the white columns in front," said Ben as he pointed to one of the stately mansions. "Perhaps have a gardener to keep everything nice and pretty. Wouldn't that be great?"

"Oh yes, and a maid to do the house work too," agreed Lily. "And speaking of work, I really must get back to Palmer Arms. I have to work tomorrow and I still need to wash and iron a few clothes."

"You're right. I have to get this horse and buggy back to Vernon Tibbs soon. He said I could use it today, so I don't want to take advantage of my new business partner."

"You haven't mentioned anything about your new business venture. How is it going?"

"So far, so good. We've bought three wagons and hired two men, both teamsters and they'll drive for us. One lives in Seattle and the other lives in Tacoma, so that works out well. And I've been able to sign contracts with two firms in Tacoma to haul freight into Seattle. One is the Evergreen Shake Mill. They have access to more cedar trees for making shakes than Seattle does, and the other contract is with the Tacoma Brewing. We're hauling kegs of beer for them to Seattle. Plus we're getting some railroad and shipping business as well."

"That sounds good."

"Yes, but I'm going to have to spend more time in the Tacoma area than up here in Seattle, and I don't like that idea."

"Oh Ben, I don't either," said Lily disappointingly. "How often will you be up here?"

"Probably just two or three times a month. When I have to sign business papers, or other things that pertain to the business. Or maybe cover for our driver up here, I really don't know for sure."

Lily was not about to lose Ben if she could help it. "When will I see you again?" she asked hopefully.

"Tell you what, I'll make sure and come up this way by the end of the month. We can get together then if you like. I could pick you up at, say eleven thirty on Sunday. Your day off, and we can go up to that new restaurant on the hill. I think it's called the High Point Restaurant. The new one that sits up on Beacon Hill."

"Yes, I've heard of it. That would be nice," said Lily quickly. Even though her weekday meals were paid for at the Rochester House, on Sundays she normally had to fare for herself unless she was invited out. This was a great opportunity and she wasn't going to miss it. Still, it was a long two and a half weeks away, but she would be with her Ben. "Yes, let's do it," she replied eagerly.

She hardy noticed that they were almost back to the Palmer Arms boarding house. She had been so enthralled with their long afternoon buggy ride, the picnic and his new business venture. "Oh my, where has this day gone! And I've still got to get ready for work tomorrow too!"

Ben stopped the horse and buggy at her stoop and helped her down from the buggy. "Lily, I really had a great time. Don't forget, we have a date on the last Sunday of this month."

"Oh Ben, I won't," she replied flirtatiously, then she turned and walked up the steps into the building. Forget, she thought to herself! How could she forget! She knew it would be on her mind every moment until the time she could be with her Ben again.

Monday morning remained clear and sunny and it brought a cheerful window of springtime to Seattle. The robins had returned from where ever they had gone for their winter exodus. Hundreds of seagulls, all dressed in white and shades of gray, flew over the docks screeching and scrounging for any scraps of fish residue left by the fishing boats.

It was clearly a beautiful time to be alive, and Lily felt all of life's passion flowing though her veins. The next morning when Russell opened the door at the Rochester House he could see that Lily was in an euphoric state. "I've never seen you look so happy! What is the big occasion? Is it your birthday or something?" he asked.

"I'm sorry to disappoint you, but the answer is none of those things. It's just a big beautiful, wonderful day," she said as she walked by his counter, then stopped and turned back towards him. "Russell, I just realized. I don't know your full name."

"It's Jewet. Russell P. Jewet, Miss Lily."

"Well Mister Russell P. Jewet," she said haughtily. "You just have to learn to smile more and enjoy the world," she added with a large smile and a winsome turn of her head as she continued on her way towards the kitchen. Lily pushed open the swinging hinged door to the kitchen and saw Angelina, and another waitress named Katy, sitting on stools having their morning coffee and donuts. Further in the back of the kitchen two of the male cooks were busy preparing food for the days expected customers.

"Good morning everyone," said Lily.

Angelina looked around at Lily. "You look too happy girl. Why are you smiling like the cat that ate the canary so early in the morning?"

"I'm just happy. That's all. Can't one enjoy a beautiful day like this?"

Angelina dunked her donut in her coffee and looked over at Katy. "It's got to be that new boy friend of hers. I've seen that look before, and it doesn't mean anything else, believe me."

"You all are just jealous," Lily replied as she took her apron off the wall hook and put it on.

"No, just a bit wiser," said Angelina as both she and Katy got up to go out front and begin the work week.

Lily carefully marked off each day on her calendar in her tiny room as she waited impatiently for the Sunday at the end of the month to arrive. The passage of each day brought her that much closer to seeing her Ben again. As that day drew near her spirits soared with more of a lilt in her walk, a smile that would not end, and the endless humming of a song about a prince and his love for a princess. Angelina and Katy started ribbing her about her upbeat attitude, but even that could not restrain her enthusiasm

Finally, at long last, the end of the month approached. On Saturday and everyone at work could tell that Lily's thoughts were upon the next day and her big date. More than once Angelina had to tell her to check on a particular customer at a certain table, or to make sure the customers had enough coffee, tea or other beverages to drink. "Girl, you have got to get this out of your system! Wake up and pay attention to what is going on around you!" she reminded her. "You're too good of a waitress to be asleep like this!"

After the long day was over Lily ate a small meal and said her goodbyes to all the staff, then gratefully left the restaurant and headed to her small room at Palmer Arms.

Lily spent a somewhat sleepless night tossing and turning in her bed, anxiously waiting for the big day to arrive. At seven thirty in the morning she finally got up and began to carefully prepare for her date. She ironed her white blouse and blue skirt, making sure all the creases were just right, styled her hair and put on her lip rouge. Then she sat down and began to wait impatiently for Ben's arrival while watching the hands on the clock move ever so slowly. She now wished she had set an earlier time for them to meet. At every sound in the street she would stand and look out the window hoping to see her Ben. It was exactly eleven thirty when he pulled up with the same horse and buggy he had used on their picnic earlier that month. She knew that he had borrowed the carriage from Vernon Tibbs again.

She quickly put on her ankle length coat, and after another quick look in the mirror to be sure she looked just right, hurried down to meet Ben. He helped her into the buggy, took the reins in hand and they rode off under a cloudy sky with a very light mist. The High Point Restaurant was located about two miles away up on Beacon hill overlooking the sound. The roadway, although wet, was in good repair and they arrived at the restaurant in about thirty minutes, just as the Sunday morning rush crowds from the neighboring churches were also beginning to arrive.

Ben stopped the carriage and handed the reins over to a stableman. "I hope you like it up here," said Ben as they got out of the buggy at the entrance to the restaurant.

"Ben, it's wonderful! What a great view. Oh my, even the Rochester House has nothing to compare with this! We are so much higher up! And even though it's cloudy, we can still see all over the sound."

Once inside, the waiter seated them at a table with a window view, and as he walked away, Lily whispered low, "This is so impressive! Are you sure you can afford it?"

"If not, we'll both have to wash dishes," he replied with a wide smile on his face.

"It just might be worth it," said Lily.

Ben ordered white wine to go with their meal of pheasant under glass. They slowly sipped at the wine, and although Lily had tasted some of the wines at the Rochester House, she was glad that they had food to go with this wine as she noticed its effect almost immediately. It wasn't bitter like the wine that they had had on their picnic, but it gave her a warm glow that seemed to be a bit too relaxing so she was careful not to drink very much. Neither of them were conscious of the time as they sat by the window looking out at the view, enjoying the food and each other at the same time. It was a perfect afternoon.

Lily finally broke the spell by asking, "How is the new freight business coming along?"

Ben looked a little disheartened. "That's one of the things I wanted to talk to you about. We seem to be doing well, but we're really not making any money yet. We're just barely covering expenses. Vernon wants me to stay in Tacoma so I can relieve one of our drivers when necessary. I'm not sure I can do that and still make the business contacts that I need to make there, but I've got to give it a try."

"Oh Ben, there's no other way?"

"Not that we can see. At least not right now."

"Does that mean I won't be seeing you?"

He reached across the table and took her hand. "Sweet little Lily, I really don't know, but I do know I'll miss you." He paused, then added, "Say, you could come with me."

She gasped, "I couldn't. It wouldn't be proper. I mean, after all, what would people think?"

"Well, we could get married first. I love you Lily," he suddenly blurted out. "I think I've always loved you. Even from the first time I saw you waiting on tables in Rosco's, then when I saw you again here in Seattle, I felt like it was fate. After we went on our haphazard picnic, I was sure that I loved you. You've been on my mind all week."

"What! Now I really don't know what to say!"

"I know this is probably a bit unexpected. Why don't you think it over for a while. I don't have to go back to Tacoma until Wednesday. That will give you time to think about it."

Lily was stunned "Oh Ben, this is so, so sudden! I don't know what to say!" Ben was certainly the man she had dreamed about, but she hadn't even considered marriage yet. This was fast, almost too fast. Her mind was reeling, "Yes, I need time to think."

She didn't remember much about the remaining part of the meal. There was a dessert, some type of custard she vaguely recalled. Ben paid the bill, and then they boarded the buggy and headed back to Palmer Arms.

The fresh air revived her. She noticed the mist was gone. The sky had cleared and nightfall would be soon approaching. It was a glorious and exciting evening to be sure! The clop, clop of the horse's hooves rang out their song in the evening.

Ben pulled up in front of her boarding house, then silently put his arm around her shoulder and pulled her close to him. She did not resist as she fell into his arms. His kiss was warm and sensual and it enveloped her to her very soul. "Oh my, this must be heaven," she thought as she gave into his kiss.

Ben slowly released his hold on her as they both sat in the buggy in the shallow light of the fading day. Ben finally spoke, "I'd better go. I've got to get back over to Vernon Tibbs early in the morning to work on one of the wagons. I'll stop back here Wednesday evening for your answer. Okay?"

"Yes, fine," said Lily trying to regain her composure.

Ben helped her down from the buggy and walked her up the stoop of the building. "Good night sweet Lily. See you on Wednesday." Then he gave her another short kiss before turning to leave.

"Good night. See you Wednesday," she repeated as she hesitated, then turned and opened the door to the building.

"Okay, and have a good night. I'll see you then," he said as he gently urged the buggy away from in front of the building. Then he was gone. The clop, clop of the horse's hooves echoing again in the early evening.

Shafts of bright sunlight abruptly intruded through the window and into Lily's room to wake her the next morning. She turned her head away, trying not to wake up. Had she been dreaming? Then she awoke with a start! No, it was still true! Her Ben had proposed to her last night! And he had said that he loved her! She remained overwhelmed by it all as she hurriedly got ready for work. She wished Anna was here so she could tell her the exciting news in person, but decided she'd write her a letter later.

Lily finished dressing and combing her hair, then applied her lip rouge. She grabbed her coat off the wall hook near the door and rushed downstairs. As she passed Lorraine Palmer, her landlord, at the foot of the stairs, she said, "Hi Mrs. Palmer. Can't talk right now, or I'll be late for work."

Lorraine stood aside and watched her go hurriedly by, then said, "Have a good day, and watch those steps. I haven't swept them off yet this morning." She noticed that her comments seemed to fall on deaf ears. "That girl!" she muttered to herself. "Always in a big hurry!"

Lily arrived at the Rochester House, tapped lightly on the door to get Russell's attention who was standing behind the counter. He put down the menu he was working on, walked over and unlocked the door. "Good morning Miss Lily."

"Ah yes, Russell. It is a good morning," she replied taking off her coat and hanging it up in the cloak room behind the counter. "Is Angelina in yet?"

"Oh yes. She's in the kitchen having her usual morning coffee. You know she can't function without it."

"Thanks Russell. I'll go back there."

Lily found both Angelina and Katy sipping at their coffee and eating their morning donuts. As she walked in Angelina looked up and remarked, "Girl, you look a little too cheerful this morning. Has it anything to do with that big date yesterday?"

"Well, it might. A little bit," she replied coyly as she took one of the fresh cake donuts off the dessert platter and dunked it into a glass of milk she had poured.

"I thought as much. Well, tell us what the big deal is."

"Yes," Katy added. "What's the big story?"

Lily looked around to make sure the cooks in the back of the kitchen could not hear, then whispered, "Ben proposed last night."

"He what?" exclaimed Angelina.

"Ssh, I don't want everyone to know," Lily said as she glanced again in the direction of the cooks.

Angelina continued with her voice a bit lower, "And what did you say?"

"I haven't yet."

"Thank God for small favors," said Angelina with a sigh of relief. "You're much too young to run off with a dandy Don."

"He's not a dandy Don! He's a respected business man."

"Mm hm. I've heard that song before. Well, what are you going to say?"

"I don't know yet. I'm thinking it over," said Lily with a little tilt of her head upward.

At that moment they heard Russell ring the bell out on the front counter. Customers were coming in and it was time to go to work. There would be more time to discuss this subject later in detail.

Mondays were almost always a bit slower and it usually allowed the waitresses to have a rest break in the afternoon. It was then that Angelina offered to talk with Lily about her proposal if she wanted to, but Lily politely declined her offer, saying that she wanted to think about the proposal by herself. She already felt quite sure she would accept Ben's offer, but she wanted to relish and languish in the joy of it. Ben was what she had always yearned for. Now it was all within her grasp, and it was all too delicious and too wonderful for mere words.

Tuesday evening after work in her room at Palmer Arms she continued to bask in the moment and to dream of a future with Ben. She opened her diary and began to write: "June 1, 1894. I have decided to accept Ben Chandler's offer of marriage."

On Wednesday evening after work Lily rushed home as quickly as she could. She hurriedly changed out of her work dress into her finest dress-up outfit, a light blue skirt along with a white long sleeve blouse with a high button collar. Then while brushing her hair out once more, she heard a light knocking at the door.

"Lily. It's Ben," said the soft voice from outside.

She walked cross the room and unlocked the door, "Please come in Ben."

Ben walked through the open doorway with a large bouquet of yellow daffodils in his hand. "Hi dear sweet Lily. Oh, these are for you."

"Oh Ben, they are so beautiful. Let me find something to put them in. I don't even have a vase in this little place, but I'm sure I can find something." She went over by her small kitchen wall shelf that was concealed by a white curtain with yellow daisies. After pushing the curtain aside she found an empty Mason canning jar and proceeded to put the flowers in it. After that she put the container on a small stand by the window. "There, this will do just fine." She stood back to admire the flowers, then leaned forward to rearrange some of the stalks. "Oh, they're just beautiful don't you think!" She turned around and saw Ben still standing. "Oh Ben, I'm sorry, please sit down. They only give us one chair in these tiny rooms. I'll just sit over here on the bed."

Ben sat down on the chair, both feet squarely on the floor and with his hands in his lap. He looked at Lily and asked slowly, "Well Lily, what have you decided? Will you marry me?"

A somber look crossed Lily's face as she decided to toy with him. "I know that you are sincere, and that any woman would be happy to have you for a husband, and you know how much I like you, but I….." She watched the expression on Ben's face darken, then said suddenly, "Yes, yes! Of course, I'll marry you!"

Ben jumped to his feet, "You little imp! You really had me going there for a minute or two! Oh Lily, this is wonderful! Oh, I love you, I love you!" Then he pulled her up into his arms and gave her a long and thrilling kiss that made her truly weak in the knees. He released her slightly, "Oh this is great! We can get a little house in Tacoma! It will just be tremendous!"

Lily began to recover her thoughts, "Ben wait! Where will we get married? I'll need a wedding dress. There's so much to do. And don't forget, I've got the job at the Rochester House."

"I've been thinking of where to have the wedding, and I think I've got it! Let's go over to Victoria on Vancouver Island. I've heard it is very picturesque. Lots of beautiful old homes with lots of flowers around them." He walked over to her calendar hanging on the wall, and ignoring the prior days she had already crossed out, began to study it. "The fifteenth is a Saturday. That's a little less than two weeks away. I know that's a little soon, but we can have it then. What do you think?"

"Oh Ben, it's so fast. I need time to think!"

"Well, unfortunately that's about the only free time I have. This new freight business is forcing me to put in many extra long hours. I'm reasonably sure I can get that weekend off, but old Vernon will not be too happy about it."

Lily noted it was the first time that he had called Vernon Tibbs 'old'. She immediately regrouped her thoughts and said, "Okay, let's do it!"

On Thursday evening, after work, Lily worked up her courage and gave notice to P.J. Concannon, owner of the Rochester House. It was extremely hard to leave as P.J. had been her benefactor. There were tears in her eyes as she remembered that he had given her a job when she was down and out and had also found her a place to live at Palmer Arms. She was very grateful that the ex-detective took it all in stride, offering his best wishes to the coming marriage and saying that she could come back to work at anytime in the future if she wanted.

Angelina and Katy took the news cheerfully as they wished her well also. However, Angelina continued to caution, "Girl, we love you here, but just you remember, the world is a big hard place out there. Also, I want to give you a warning. I've heard that Ron Appleton has been trying to find out why you've been avoiding him. I'd watch out for him if I were you. And remember too girl, if you pass by this way again, you stop in and see us." She gave Lily a big hug adding, "Now, if you should ever need help, you stop by and see me personally."

The wedding was held in Victoria on Vancouver Island, British Columbia at the Church of the Almighty on June fifteenth at one o'clock in the afternoon, only one hour after the ferry from Seattle docked. It was a whirlwind trip that left the newlyweds just one honeymoon night before catching a ferry back to Seattle on Sunday morning.

Upon docking in Seattle they returned to the Palmer Arms boarding house and picked up Lily's two remaining suitcases from her room, then proceeded to the train depot to catch the train back to Tacoma. Ben had already located and rented a small two bedroom house with a barn and garden area on the out skirts of Fife, which was a small farming community on the east side of Tacoma. The rental was on the north end of Algona road that ran south across the wide valley.

The happy couple soon settled into a very quiet domestic life style. Lily remained at home striving to become a traditional and loving housewife while Ben continued working the Tacoma market for C & T Hauling Company. He would normally get up at five thirty every morning and rekindle the fire in the kitchen. Next, Lily would fix him a quick breakfast and pack him a lunch for the day. By six thirty Ben had harnessed the gray to the buggy, which he had bought from Vernon Tibbs shortly after starting the new business, then he would ride into Tacoma.

After making sure all was in good order at the warehouse, he would start on his rounds to pick up and deliver the morning freight. Coming back in around eleven in the morning, they would load out one or two wagons for Seattle. Later that evening the teamster would off load at Vernon Tibbs' warehouse. That evening, or early the next morning, the same driver would load produce for the return trip to Tacoma. Usually after the driver had left for Seattle Ben would arrange the other incoming freight for local and out of town deliveries. After that he would sort through the paperwork, putting the local bills of lading in order, and put aside the completed freight bills to be sent up to Vernon Tibbs. This meant he usually got home about eight or nine o'clock each evening.

Lily was not an accomplished cook, but she worked diligently trying to improve to make her Ben happy and comfortable. After Ben left in the mornings, she would heat more water on the wood stove to wash the dishes and possibly wash some clothes too. Although she had washed her own clothes at Palmer Arms she found it very hard to keep Ben's heavy work clothes clean and in good repair. Her arms would ache from using a wash board in the tub of sudsy water trying to get all the stains out of them. After hanging the clothes out to dry, she would clean their small house. When wild flowers were available she would put them in a small vase on the table to brighten the room. She tried to make sure make there was enough wood and kindling cut up for that day and coming morning. By then it was time try to prepare a meal that could be ready at the approximate time when Ben would arrive home.

She tried hard to look her best for Ben when he returned home. Her hair was neatly combed and she always tried to wear a clean and pretty dress for him. Later she found a book about crocheting and began to teach herself how to crochet, but soon discovered it a bit boring. Besides, after preparing the meals, washing and mending their clothes, plus other chores, she didn't really have the time for other mundane tasks.

Their nearest neighbor was almost one mile away so it was rare that Lily got to see anyone. The only saving grace was that the road to Seattle was near by so she could occasionally see people in buggies or wagons pass. Even that soon became dreary and quite monotonous. But, when they were together, they enjoyed their precious time alone.

Summer seemed to end so quickly and almost before they realized it, fall was upon them. The onset of September brought shorter days and a cooling of the temperatures, but it was still very comfortable outdoors. It was typical of this time of year, crisp sunny days and little rain.

Ben worked part of every Saturday catching up on paperwork at the warehouse which he sent each Monday via the freight wagon to Seattle. The remaining portion of Saturday he used to purchase feed for their work horses. If any time was left in the day, he would use it and maybe part of Sunday, to buy hay, wood, and food for personal use. All items that usually had to be hauled home on Sunday to stock up for the coming season.

The ensuing weeks seemed to fly by for the busy young couple. Very quickly it became the time of year when all the vine maple leaves turn to shades of gold intermingled with varying degrees of reds bursting forth to bring the landscape alive with color. The reds were more apparent as they were accented by the back ground of the green fir trees. At the same time all the orchards full of various fruit trees and other surrounding deciduous trees join in to show their brilliant yellow and browns. This time of year is often called 'Indian Summer'. It's when the warm summer sunshine forgets to fade, but instead remains until the start of the winter season. The leaves soon drop to the ground, wither and dry, then make a crunching sound when stepped on. As the cold weather finally arrives, morning frosts appear, and one's breath is visible in the cool crisp air.

Even as the days shortened, the freight business kept Ben very busy and he seldom got home before dark. He was beginning to become disenchanted with the low pay he was getting. Their budget was very tight and it worried him that they had put nothing aside. He began to wonder why he had not received any of the profit moneys that Vernon Tibbs had promised they would split. In early December Ben took a freight load to Seattle to ask Vernon about the money situation.

He arrived in Seattle at four o'clock in the afternoon and after unloading the freight destined for that area, the warehouse crew helped Ben load the produce that had to go to Tacoma on the return trip. After that task was completed he went into Vernon Tibbs' office in the back corner of the building.

Vernon looked up as Ben knocked lightly at his door. "Ben, come on in. It's good to see you. Glad you stopped in, as I wanted to review things with you." Vernon reached into the top drawer of his desk and pulled out a large heavy bound ledger titled 'C & T Hauling Company'. "Have a seat. We need to go over this."

Ben sat down on the hard oak chair in front of the desk. "That's why I'm here. I've got a few questions. To be blunt, I'm wondering when I'll be getting that bonus you promised long ago."

Vernon thumbed through the pages in the large book until he came to a section marked 'Profit and Loss'. Then he flipped through the pages until he came to a statement dated December 1st, 1895. "Look at this figure." He pointed at the bottom of the page. "Down here where it shows 'net profit'.

Ben's eyes passed over the top of the page where the expenses were entered and looked down at the bottom of the page. "Yes, I see it. It says, 'eighteen dollars and thirty cents', but I don't understand how there can be so little profit after all of our hard work."

Vernon leaned back in his chair. "Okay let me explain it. You're working hard to handle the cargo, that I know. Once a week you send me the bills of lading that I have to put the freight rate on and extend out, then mail out the bills to our customers. Now, one of our main problems is that we have to be competitive. That means I have to put down a competitive rate so that our customers will continue to use our company to ship their goods." He waited to see Ben's reaction, then continued, "I've been watching our overhead very closely, so I know we can't trim anywhere. Salaries alone take the biggest bite and collections have not been very good in todays economy. You read the papers. The whole country is in an economic depression."

"Yes, I've read a bit about it. Times are difficult, I know, but...." Ben tried to gather his thoughts.

Vernon continued, "And right now we have a major competitor, and that is the new railroad between Tacoma and Seattle. Frankly Ben, they are killing us!"

Stunned, Ben leaned back in his chair. "Well, what can we do? Does this mean we're going bankrupt or out of business?

"No, it's tight, but not that desperate. Remember this is December, the slowest time of the year. In the spring things will pick up. We've made good strides so far. Our wagons and pulling stock are finally paid for. That means, that when spring comes and business picks up again, we should have some extra money in the coffers. Then I'll be able to pay you better. I'm sorry, but we just don't have it right now. I hope you understand."

It was a crushing blow for Ben as he had hoped to use the money to pay off some accounts in Tacoma. Namely a small account with Herb's Market and another bill with Puget Sound Stables for shoeing and harness work for the gray he had bought.

On the trip back to Tacoma the next morning he worried about telling Lily the bad news. To make matters worse it had begun to rain. A bone chilling rain was blowing in ever so slightly from the west off the Pacific Ocean and across the Puget Sound. It made the trip seem excessively long. He arrived in Tacoma completely numb and soaking wet with the load of produce. By the time the wagon was unloaded and he returned home it was after seven in the evening. He still had to unharness the gray, put her in the small barn and feed her, before going inside to the welcoming warmth of the house.

Lily heard him arrive and quickly poured a bucket of warm water so he could soak his sore and tired feet. For good measure she added more wood to the stove to help Ben thaw out from his cold day's work. Soon she heard the stomp of his boots on the outside step where he was pounding mud off his boots before he came inside.

She opened the door. "Come on in. I can clean all the mud off later. You need to dry off and get warm."

Thankfully, Ben stepped into the warm room. "Thanks. Boy, it's really getting cold out there," he said as he began to take off his heavy wet clothes. "I'm not looking forward to the winter snows, that's for sure."

Quickly Ben stripped down and put on fresh dry clothes Lily had laid out for him, then sat down to soak his tired feet in the warm water. "Thanks Lily, you're a treasure, and I mean it."

"You get warm and comfortable and I'll heat up your supper. I've got potatoes, gravy, a small salad and some left over chicken. It will be ready shortly." Soon Lily had everything warmed up and on the table for him. "Okay, come on over here and sit down and eat your meal. Now, tell me, how did your meeting go with Vernon Tibbs?"

Ben scooted his chair up to the table, "Not so good." As he began eating he patiently tried to explain to Lily why he hadn't gotten any bonus money. "I guess Vernon is right. Times are tight and now that the railroad has been extended to Seattle, it has been taking some of our freight business. But like he said, when spring comes we'll be making up for it," Ben said trying to sound optimistic.

"I don't quite understand how you can work so hard and put in all these long hours, then when springs comes, it is supposed to get busier. How can you work any longer than you are now? It just doesn't seem to make any sense. Something doesn't seem right."

A tired and weary Ben replied, "Don't worry sweet Lily. It will all work out." At least he hoped it would.

The following week the first snow came, a light blow of soft flakes that slowly drifted down to the ground covering the fields, roads and green fir trees with a brilliant blanket of white. It was a pretty sight if one does not have to work out in the mud and frost which quickly follows in the wake of the first snow storm of the winter season.

The short days passed slowly, yet quickly. December flew by in a rush as the days melted in a blur of long hours of work. Slowly Lily was finding out that being a housewife was not the bed of roses she had expected. Housework and being confined all day was extremely boring and mundane after the fast pace of work at her old job at the Rochester House. Before, right after work, she had been able to take a walk and enjoy the views along the docks on the waterfront. It had been relaxing and stimulating at the same time. Due to the long hours Ben was working and short dark days, the household chores were becoming oppressive.

Christmas was not the great day she had hoped for. It started out as a cold and blustery day and continued that way most of the day. Ben had put up a small tree in the corner of their living room, but it just didn't quite have enough decorations. Money was short because the hauling business was down at this time of the year. Thus the presents they exchanged were somewhat meager. Socks and a new shirt for him and a sweater and some cooking utensils for her. Lily was very depressed as she remembered the happy Christmas's she had had at her parent's home, and wondered if her mother had ever received the sewing cabinet that her father had promised. At least in Seattle at the Rochester House, there was the excitement of season and one was buoyed up by the other people around. Now, even with Ben trying to comfort her, she felt isolated.

Friday, the ninth of January, Ben arrived home early much to Lily's concern and delight. "Why are you home so early," she asked as she brushed her hair back from the side of her face and in the process got some white baking flour on the side of her cheek. "I haven't started to clean up. Supper's not even ready yet."

"Don't be concerned. It's your day. Don't you remember, it's your birthday!"

"Oh Ben, you remembered! How sweet. Oh, I love you; you big oaf!" she said as she reached up and wrapped her arms around his neck and gave him a deep welcome home kiss. "And what did you get for me?" she asked in a quiet seductive voice.

"Nothing, not a thing," he replied.

She continued to stand with her arms around him, their bodies pressed close together, "I don't believe you."

Ben took her hands down. "Well, maybe I did get you something. Let me go back out to the buggy and see."

He came back into the house with two presents wrapped in brilliant shades of blue adorned with striking white bows. He put them on the table, then handed her a rose colored envelope.

"Oh Ben, what is this? I know, let me guess. It's a check for five thousand dollars!" she gushed joyfully.

As she opened the envelope, he answered, "No, it's only for one thousand dollars!"

She read the card aloud, "For my dear sweet Lily on her nineteenth birthday. May the succeeding years bring you as much happiness as you have brought to me, All my love, Ben." She took a deep breath and allowed each word to soak in.

"Oh, it's absolutely wonderful. Thank you," She turned to look at the presents on the table, "And what do we have here?"

"Not as much as you deserve."

"Oh, I doubt that," Lily replied as she reached for the larger package and began to open it. Inside the box were two more packages. She took out the larger one of the two and opened it. "Oh, it's a new winter coat! And I really need it! My other coat is far too light for winter, but when I lived in the city and was close to work I didn't really need a real heavy coat like I do now." She put the new coat on a chair and picked up the smaller package. "This is heavier. Did you buy me a pound of lead?" She quickly opened up the smaller box to discover it was a pair of high laced shoes to match the new coat. "Ben, how thoughtful. These will look good together. I almost can't wait to go outside now."

"I hope you like them. A saleslady at Jacobs Clothing store helped me pick them out."

"And what is in this small light blue package?"

"I don't know."

"Ben, you are a big fibber!"

Lily tore open the smaller package to discover a silver heart shaped locket and chain carefully wrapped in two brand new laced trimmed hankies. She laid the hankies aside as she held the locket and chain set up to her neck, then turned to look in the small mirror that hung above the kitchen sink. "Oh, this is so beautiful, but I don't know where I can wear this. It looks so elaborate."

"Hopefully someday, we'll be able to afford to go out and dine in style. Maybe even buy one of those big homes like the kind we admired up on Queen Anne Hill over there in Seattle."

She threw her arms around his neck again, "Oh Ben, that would be so wonderful!" Then she released him a little bit, leaned back and asked, "And what do we buy this fancy home with?"

"Hopefully Mister Vernon Tibbs will come through with some of the bonus money he promised. But so far, as you know, all we've received are our standard paychecks for myself and our drivers. But he said to be patient and after expenses get paid we'll get a large pay increase in the way of a bonus based upon the profit we make."

"Any idea of just when that may be?"

"Sorry Honey, I don't."

"Well, right now we are getting by, and that is the important thing," said Lily cheerfully. "I'm sure it will all work out." Then she leaned forward and gave Ben a long hard passionate kiss. "Thanks for remembering my birthday," she whispered in his ear.

That evening and much of the night was spent enjoying the sensual pleasures of a married couple. However, what Lily did not know was that Ben still had to pay for her birthday gifts. He had hoped that the bonus money from the company would have come through so he could have paid for them outright, but it had not happened.

With the passing of January and February came March with its blowing rains to melt the snows, which complicated things by making roads a muddy quagmire. Slowly, but surely, the sun began to show through the cloudy skies more frequently and by April, spring flowers had begun to bud out, bringing a cheerful glow to the landscape. Business was starting to pick up again and once again Ben was putting in long hours at work.

"Lily Honey, I think it's about time that I went up to talk with Vernon again. Business is up and we need to put on more help. Plus, we need that bonus money he promised."

Lily had gotten over most of her winter depression. "It would be nice if it comes through, but I'm not counting on it. Remember what happened last time when you asked for the money."

"Well, this time it will be different," said Ben firmly. "I've had it with these long hours and little pay! I'll just plain quit if he doesn't come through this time! I really mean it!"

The following Monday Ben again replaced his regular teamster driver and took the load of material up to Seattle. After the goods were off loaded and a new load of produce loaded for the return trip, he knocked on Vernon Tibbs's office door.

The gray haired Vernon sat at his desk with his dark billed visor cap on. As usual he had been poring over pages of bills of lading, pricing and extending the figures. Hearing Ben's knock, he looked up. "Come on in Ben," he acknowledged with a wave of his hand as he leaned back in his chair, "I needed a break anyway. What brings you up this way today?"

Ben sat down in the old chair in front of Vernon's desk and took a deep breath. "Frankly Vernon, I'm worn out. I was up here last September as you know. You said that when things picked up you'd give me some extra money. I can't put in any more hours than I'm already doing, and besides that, we need more help at the Tacoma warehouse. We just can't handle the load anymore. Dammit Vernon, I've just pretty much had it."

"Well, let's take a look at the books," said Vernon as he reached into his desk for the C & T Hauling Company ledger. Quickly he opened it up to the Profit and Loss section. "I just finished balancing everything out a couple of days ago. I'll show you the latest figures."

"Figures be damned! I need more money and I need more help!"

Vernon held up his palm, "Hold on. Calm down." Then he looked down at the page in front of him. "Ah yes, here it is." He ran his finger to the bottom line. "Yes, we are doing better, but we've just barely started turning a profit and as you can see that figure is small. Only one hundred and twelve dollars, but improving that is for sure."

"I really don't care what that book says. I have to have more money or I'm leaving. It's just not worth it to me to work these kind of hours anymore."

"Okay, okay Ben. Look, you saw the figures. Tell you what I'll do." He closed the ledger and leaned back in his chair. "I'll give you fifty dollars right now, and you can take another forty into consideration to hire another man down there. That will leave us twenty two dollars to the good." Then he added, attempting to appease him further, "Things will continue to improve, and Ben there will be more money coming, but I think you can see that is all I can do now."

Ben knew he had not gained much, but he was desperate for the money. Grudgingly he agreed, "Okay Vernon, but you know this is not very much money. I think I deserve more."

"And you're right!" Vernon quickly added as he knew he had made a good bargain. He reached in his top left drawer of his desk and retrieved a checkbook. "I'll make out your check right now. Things will get better, I promise."

Ben wondered how good the promise really was as he accepted the small fifty dollar bonus check.

The trip back to Tacoma the next day was delayed by a broken wagon wheel that had to be replaced on the wagon that had been loaded out the night before. Somehow Ben and the others had not noticed that four of the wooden spokes were broken. Now they had no choice but to jack up the right rear of the wagon and replace the wheel with a spare they had in the warehouse. By the time this was completed, it was seven o'clock in the morning before he was able to leave the Seattle warehouse.

On the long trip back to Tacoma Ben had time to think over his meeting with Vernon Tibbs and he began to wonder about the financial figures. Possibly he should not have been so rash. Maybe he should have taken the time to look at the expense portion of the Profit and Loss form more closely. He began to ask himself a number of questions. How much was Vernon taking out of the business for his wages? And just what kind, and how much, were the warehouse costs? Could any of these costs be actually inflated? Would it be possible that Vernon could be taking out a sizable sum of money leaving just enough to show practically no profit for the period? These were troublesome questions brought to mind.

It was dark by the time Ben got off loaded in Tacoma, hitched up his gray mare and headed for home. A mile after crossing the Puyallup River he could occasionally see a light shining from a window in their small house. It reminded him of a beacon that called him home, and at that point, he thoroughly understood when sailors used the word 'homing beacon'.

Lily heard the buggy come by the house and knew Ben was putting up the gray in the barn. She crossed her fingers and hoped that Ben had brought home good news, then she heard his footsteps coming up to the back door.

A weary Ben opened the door and entered. "Hi sweet Lily," he smiled wanly. "Finally made it. Still a might nippy out there," he said as he took off his heavy coat and hung it on a wall peg.

Lily wiped her hands on her apron and stopped setting the table as she walked up to Ben and gave him a long kiss. "Missed you, and I'm sure glad you are home."

"Missed you too, I made it okay. Sorry I'm later than usual but I had a little delay coming out of Seattle. Had to replace a wagon wheel before I left. Didn't notice it was broken until this morning. Actually it wasn't broken, just cracked in a couple of places, same difference though."

"Come on. Sit down at the table and rest. You can tell me how things went while you eat. I've just about got everything ready."

Ben sat down and began to unlace his boots. "Well, the big thing is that I got some of the bonus money. Not much, but some."

Hesitantly Lily asked, "How much?"

"Only fifty dollars, but I did get the okay to hire on an extra man here at Tacoma, and that should make my work an awful lot easier."

Like Ben, Lily was disappointed in the small amount, but tried not to show it. "Well, it's fifty dollars more than we had before," she said trying to sound optimistic. "And I'm really glad that you can put on some extra help. Maybe I'll get to see a bit more of you now." She delayed a moment, then said, "Ben, I can help. Let me go back to work. I can talk to Rosco in Tacoma, perhaps he would give me a job again as a waitress."

"No Lily, we'll be okay now. Just be patient."

The past months of confinement had Lily's patience starting to wear thin. Things weren't supposed to be this hard. Then she asked, "Did Vernon say when there will be any more bonus money?"

"No, not really, but next time I'm going to take a bit more time and ask some questions about the book keeping figures."

"Oh, is there something wrong?"

"I'm not sure. I just want to look at the figures a lot closer next time, 'cause I do have a few questions now."

Lily recognized that she would have to wait until 'next time'. Ben was tired, and it would serve no good to go on about it, so she changed the subject. "Ben, go ahead and eat before things get cold. Tomorrow's another day."

Now that Ben had Vernon's approval, he was determined to quickly hire a new man. There were a lot of unemployed men that hung out at the Tacoma railroad yards looking for work, so he had a vast choice of men to pick from. After careful deliberation he picked a young Norwegian boy named Einnar Torglesen who appeared to have a quick mind and was strong enough to handle the heavy freight involved.

The economy remained relatively flat during this period of time, but due to the hard work that Ben had put in, C & T Hauling continued to show a modest increase in business. The additional manpower had an almost immediate impact and for the first time in eight months Ben was able to come home in the daylight hours. He said it seemed as if he had gained a free day, yet they were still not able to put any moneys aside. There was enough money to pay the monthly rent, the food bill, to make small payments at the harness shop, and against the charges at Jacobs Clothing in Tacoma, but nothing was ever left over.

It was a frustrating time for the both of them. Lily continued to ask Ben to allow her to look for work, as she explained that she could ride into Tacoma with him in the morning, do her job, and meet him after work to ride home together. However, Ben remained stubborn on this issue as he felt that his wife's place was in the home and slowly a strain began to creep into their relationship, although neither one seemed to openly acknowledge it. Both attempted to carry on as if everything was smooth and comfortable.

The months continued to fly by. September was suddenly upon them and they had not gained, nor had they lost. They were merely continuing to hold their own. Lily wanted to yell out in frustration over their situation, but at the same time she realized that many others were in far worse shape then they were, so she held back her tongue.

Ben was now able to get out of the warehouse to pursue other freight business. He was slowly building up contacts with some of the ships coming into the harbor. As a result he was getting small orders to deliver, but the bulk of the material was still being off loaded and shipped by railroad. However, he was also establishing contacts with a lot of the personnel that worked on the vessels and he began to get tips on what types of cargo was coming in and on which ships. This often allowed him to be first in asking for that business.

One of these ships was the Excelsior that had just come in from Alaska, and from one of these contacts who handled government mail, Ben learned that there had been a mineral strike in Alaska. Ben mentally filed away the information as he had learned that every tiny scrap of information might help him later in business.

A chill in October burst upon the land with its display of bright autumn colors, the golds and various shades of red again changing the color of the northwest. These colors were especially apparent after the taller evergreen fir trees had been logged, thereby giving room for the maples and alders to flourish.

At the end of October Ben made another run to Seattle to discuss business with Vernon. This time when Vernon dug out the black ledger, Ben carefully reviewed the expense figures and asked Vernon about each of the charges listed. Each and every time Vernon had a reasonable answer for the amounts posted. The bottom line of the Profit and Loss statement did not reflect any great earnings. Still Ben had lingering doubts about the figures. It was only a net profit of ninety-one dollars and thirty cents, and Vernon immediately wrote Ben a check for one half of that amount, forty-five dollars and sixty five cents. Again, it was far less than what Ben had expected, but at least it would pay off the remaining charges at the harness shop and at Jacobs Clothing.

As another winter approached Lily began canning fruit. There was one lonely peach tree by their rental house and from that tree she was able to put up ten quarts of peaches. They bought cherries and pears and she put up nearly fifteen jars of each. It was a hot tedious task that she really didn't care for, but she knew it had to be done. Ben dug a shallow root cellar, but he hit water at five feet depth, so he had to stop and line the bottom with stone, hoping that the winter water table would not rise any higher. After putting in some rough cut shelving they stored the fall harvest of potatoes and apples in it.

In late November two ships came into the harbor. One was the Portland from San Francisco and the other was the Excelsior which had just completed another run from the Alaska territory. Ben decided to meet the Excelsior again as he had more contacts on that ship. His contacts paid off, and he ended up with two freight loads. Both destined for the local market and both would be easy to handle. It was one of his better days.

After the arrangements were made and cargo papers signed, he went by the mail room to visit his information source. His friend told him that the mineral strike he had mentioned back in September was really a gold or silver strike. No one really knew exactly how big or where it was, but he told Ben that there would be a need for a freight business up there to haul supplies to the mines and suggested it might be something that he might want to look into.

Ben thought about that information all afternoon and during the evening ride home. That night he mentioned to Lily, "I heard from one of the men on the Excelsior that there has been a gold or silver strike up in Alaska and he suggested that I check it out."

"Gold!"

"Wait, it's not the minerals I'm interested in because no one really knows at this point how much gold, or silver, or anything else is up there. What I'm being told is that there are many stories starting to come out of Alaska, and that there might be a good opportunity to make some good money there."

"I don't understand?"

"Lily, It's the freight I'm thinking of."

"What?"

"From what I hear, there are no real freight companies up there right now. The ships have been going into a town called Skagway and they just off load on the tide flats, and that's where the owners are picking up their freight. The point is that if there were a hauling company there, it could be a profitable thing."

"Oh Ben, I don't know. Are you actually thinking about going up there?"

"I really don't know. I've been giving it a lot of thought though. If I sold out my half of C & T Hauling to Vernon, I could raise some money. But there are a lot of other things involved. Like bank financing, money drafts, money for passage. I don't know what all is needed, or even how long it will take to put it all together."

"Oh, it sounds so complicated."

"I'm thinking that it is. Horses or oxen will probably have to be brought here and shipped up there. I doubt if wagons can be bought up there either, so they would have to be shipped in as well. I'd be busy, that is for sure." He paused to take a sip of his coffee, "Oh Lily, it would be some adventure!"

"And just where is this big town of Skagway?"

"As near as I can determine it's in the southern part of Alaska, right along the coast, at least that is what I've been told. That's where I'd probably start up a business. One thing for sure though, I don't think we should mention this to anyone. If it is a huge thing we could get in on the ground floor and we might finally make a decent living for a change." He sat his coffee cup down and leaned back in his chair and put his hands behind his head, "Anyway, it's something we can think about over the winter because we couldn't possibly go up there until early next year."

"Oh Ben, I just don't know."

December was quickly upon them. The freight business had slowed again so Ben used the extra time to buy four cords of seasoned Douglas Fir firewood for the winter and proceeded to cut it up to fit their two stoves. After it was cut he stacked it all neatly under a lean-to attached to the barn. Next he took the pieces with the most pitch that he had put aside and cut it all up into kindling. He ended up with a kindling pile about four feet high and four feet long.

Again Christmas was not an extravagant affair, as they had learned from the previous year how difficult it was to pay off the charges for those gifts. As a result Lily made a chocolate cake along with three mincemeat and three apple pies that they might enjoy during the holidays. She did get Ben a new flannel winter shirt with the money that she had carefully hoarded from her house budget. He brought her a white high neck blouse as he had noticed that her other one was becoming frayed.

Unlike last year when they spent New Year's Eve alone, this year they were invited to the home of Bob and Laura Crawford who were their nearest neighbors. Bob passed out some hard cider for the adults while their four children played in the kitchen, bobbing for apples. Lily enjoyed the cider, but she missed the mild pleasant taste of a good wine that P.J. had served at the Rochester House during the festive occasions held there. Both Ben and Lily laughed about the cider later as they recalled it was far better than the red wine Ben had bought in Seattle when they had gone for their buggy ride along the shoreline.

On January the ninth Lily became twenty years old, and in spite of their slightly improved financial situation, times were still tight. To celebrate the occasion, Bob and Laura Crawford had them over for dinner and it was a welcome relief for Lily not to have to prepare a complete meal for a change.

The first snow of the season came in the middle January of 1897. Before that they had the usual continuing northwest rainstorms that seemed to last forever, so the snow was a welcome sight. It covered the wet dreary gray landscape and the muddy roads making everything look bright, clean and pretty. For the children and those who didn't have to work outside in the weather, it was a playground of winter delight.

Ben and Lily even took time to take a Sunday sleigh ride in the Crawford's sleigh and Lily's impish side showed itself as she stuffed snow down Ben's back. It was one of the very few times that they got to laugh and enjoy themselves together as Ben was usually too busy working.

In March the Excelsior docked again in Tacoma and Ben was on hand to pursue any business that he could find. He was becoming an expert at negotiating and once again he had good luck in getting small profitable contracts to be delivered to the surrounding area. Before he left the docks, he made another stop to visit his mail room contact. This time the information he gathered was far more specific.

There had been a large gold strike in the Northwest Territory of Canada called the Yukon. To get there, one had to book passage and go up to the northern part of Alaska, then unload and get a steamer to go up the Yukon River to a small town called Dawson in the center of the gold fields. However, the drawback to this route was that the Yukon river could only be navigated for about four months each year after the spring thaw.

It was suggested the cheapest way would be to book passage to Dyea, located about nine miles from Skagway, on the lower coast. The mailman said he had heard of a trail there the Indians use to hike to Dawson. He further explained that they had dropped off inventory for two men who had a trading post at Dyea. This he was sure would be the future major shipping point for most of the material going to the gold fields.

Ben was very elated to get this news and as soon as he arrived home he told Lily what he had learned.

Again Lily was hesitant. "I just don't know. How can there be a lot of business in this town of Dyea if there is only one little trading post?"

"That's really not the point now. Remember what we heard about the California gold rush. Thousands and thousands of people came to Sutter's Mill in California searching for their fortunes, but the only ones who made any money were the business people who supplied the services. That's why, if we are first in, we'll be making the money this time."

"Oh Ben, I'm excited about it too, but let me sleep on it. It's kind of overwhelming. I need time to think about it."

"Okay, but we have to decide soon because we have to raise the money, buy wagons and livestock, and everything else we will need, and all this would take time."

Lily spent a restless night thinking about making this major change in their lives, but by the next morning she had made up her mind. "Ben, let's wait until we have further proof of this discovery. If it turns out like you say, then let's go for it!"

On July seventeenth, 1897, the steamer Portland docked in Seattle amid shouts of a gold strike in the Alaskan Yukon. To prove it, the steamer had on board seven hundred thousand dollars worth of gold. Now, the word was out and the newspapers in both Tacoma and Seattle were flooded with articles about the fabulous find. No one talked of anything else. Bankers said it would bring a big boost to the sluggish economy which further excited investors and others who wished to cash in on easy profits. The papers all printed glowing articles about how gold could be picked up right off the ground.

Ben left work when he heard conversations about the huge strike and headed straight for home. He barged into the house yelling, "It's been confirmed! They've hit gold big time in Alaska! Dammit Lily, we may have missed out on our big chance! Why didn't you believe me when I said earlier that we could get rich up there!"

"Oh no. It's actually true!" Lily grabbed a chair and eased herself down into it. She tried to make amends for her reluctance to believe him earlier. "I'm sorry, I just found it hard to believe that the stories were anything more than pipe dreams."

"Pipe dreams, hell! They're bringing in thousands of dollars of gold into Seattle off the Portland, and I just heard that down in San Francisco the Excelsior is unloading even more right now!"

She tried to calm him down. "Okay, we can still go up there. We'll be able to start up a good business now that the word is out and lots of people will be headed that way. It's not too late, in fact it may work out even better as there will be incoming freight right away. You won't have to work so hard to get shipments of freight." She let that sink in and continued, "Now then, what do we need to get started?"

At that point Ben collected his wits and sat down as Lily got out a pad and pencil and began making up a list of things to do first. "Number one, sell off Ben's half of the business. Number two, check on fare costs to Dyea. Number three.........."

The following day Ben took off from work and rode up to Seattle on the train which was a lot quicker than one of his freight wagons. He got off at the downtown depot and walked the remaining seven blocks to the C & T Hauling office. Vernon was sitting in his office sipping on a cup of coffee and reading the the Seattle Post-Intelligencer which was emblazoned with articles about the gold discovery. Ben hesitated, then knocked on his office door.

Vernon looked up, a little surprised, "Come in Ben. What brings you up here this time of the month?"

"Got to go over something with you."

Vernon lay his newspaper aside on the corner of his cluttered desk. "Well, go ahead. What is on your mind?"

"I've decided to sell out my part of the business. I'm going to head up north to Alaska."

"What! Have you got gold fever? You can't be serious!"

"I assure you I am serious. I've been thinking about making this move for some time now, and I'm going to do it!"

"My God Ben, you can't just up and leave me like this! I need time to find a replacement."

"I've been thinking about that, and that new young Einnar Torglesen I hired over a year ago is doing a great job. He'll be able to handle the job for you with no problems."

"Ben, are you sure about this? You won't change your mind?"

"No, my mind's made up. Just pay me for my half of the business. The way I figure it, I'd guess the business is worth about five thousand dollars. If you'll pay me twenty-five hundred, I'll be on my way."

Vernon sat still for a moment, then spoke, "Ben, you don't own half of the business. Our agreement was that I put up the money and the expertise and we split the profits. There was never any ownership involved."

Ben was devastated. "That can't be. You always said we were equal partners."

"And we were, when it came to sharing the profits Ben, but that was it. Let me get the original papers out of the safe, and I'll show you."

Ben remained absolutely stunned and quiet at this news as Vernon got up and went to the safe at the end of the room. He spun the combination dial back and forth, opened the safe and pulled out a document titled "Business Agreement". He brought the document back to Ben, "Here. Read this. It's not a partnership deed. It's a business agreement."

Ben looked through the two page agreement and had to agree that the papers he had signed indeed were not any type of ownership papers, but was merely an agreement 'to split any and all profits equally'. He silently handed the papers back to Vernon who laid them on top of the newspaper he had been reading.

They both sat quietly, then Vernon spoke first, "Ben, look I can see you have your heart set on this Alaska thing. You've been a good employee and a big help in getting this little business off the ground in Tacoma." He leaned forward across his desk, "Tell you what I'll do. I'll write you a check for five hundred dollars. That ought to buy you and Lily passage up there and allow for a few extras."

Although Ben was thoroughly disappointed, he recognized that Vernon was really trying to help. "Thanks Vernon, I do appreciate this. Sorry I misunderstood our arrangement."

Vernon got the checkbook out of his desk and began to write. "Ben, that's okay. Maybe this will help you get started up north, and if you ever get back this way, I can always find a place for a good man."

A dejected Ben left the C & T Hauling building. His mind reeling from this sudden financial set back. He had quit his job and there was no going back now. His bed had been made. He had figured that it would cost him about two thousand dollars to book passage for themselves, the wagons, livestock and fodder required. The extra money he had counted on was to buy some ground with a barn and a small cabin for himself and Lily. What was he going to do now, he wondered.

He was still devastated when he broke the news to Lily later. Lily however, thought about the problem for a while, than smiled and said, "Look at the bright side. We can sell the buggy, then take the gray you bought from Tibbs with us. That's one less animal to buy. Didn't you once say that passage runs about one hundred and fifty dollars for each of us?"

"Yes."

Well, that's only three hundred dollars, plus one hundred to ship each head of livestock, plus what food and hay we take. We can just about stretch it out to make it. And don't forget, we can still get something for the buggy."

Ben was starting to come alive again. It might be possible, he realized. "We can get about fifty dollars for the buggy. That will help, and I'm sure that I can get a loan from the bank, or some one else, for a couple of hundred more. I think we can make it!"

Lily sat quietly for a moment, "I remember a banker who owned the church building where my folks went to church up on McKinley Avenue. Let me think." She closed her eyes for a moment trying call up old memories. "He owns the New Line Bank. Oh, what was his name?" Again she closed her eyes and thought back. "I know, I know, his name is Stanley Harrison. That's it, I'm sure of it!"

"Stanley Harrison, hmm. Don't know him. Now that I think about it, I don't know any bankers at all. Vernon Tibbs did all the money handling through his banker friends in Seattle, and I have never met any of those guys either."

"I don't know if Mister Harrison would remember me. I only saw him in passing when the church elders had business with him. But, I think it's worth a try Ben if we both went in to see him together."

The next morning at nine Ben and Lily were the first customers waiting to get in when the New Line Bank on Pacific Avenue opened for business. They presented themselves to a bespectacled and slightly balding clerk behind the tellers window and asked to see Stanley Harrison. After inquiring about their need to see Mister Harrison, he left his station and knocked on the dark mahogany door marked 'President' at the rear of the bank.

Soon he returned, "Mr. Harrison will see you now." He motioned with his hand, "Follow me please," as he ushered them into the banker's spacious office lined with, what seemed to Lily, a complete library of books.

A very tall man with black hair and heavy dark eyebrows stood up from behind his desk. "Welcome." He pointed to the chairs in front of his desk. "Please have a chair. Now, what can I do for you today?"

Lily took the lead, and smiling in her most pleasant way, explained their need to borrow two hundred dollars.

The banker listened carefully to her as he leaned back in his swivel chair. Finally he bent forward, "Now let me get this straight, you want me to loan you two hundred dollars so you can go to Alaska to find gold?"

"Oh no," said Lily quickly. "My husband is starting up a freight business there, and he has the experience. He started, and has run successfully, the C & T Hauling business here in the Tacoma. We, he and I, know how to do this," she added as she stretched the truth a bit. "We have five hundred dollars already, and we'll sell our buggy for a bit more. We just need another two hundred to buy a wagon and another horse or two."

The banker sat quietly thinking about the request, then he asked, "Mrs. Chandler, isn't George Millet your father?"

"Yes, he is," Lily said with a gulp in her throat, hoping the banker would not go any further in this direction.

Mister Harrison nodded, "I thought so. He's a good man. An elder in the church if I recall right."

"Yes, he is," she replied again, not really knowing if this was still true or not.

The banker was busy making up his mind. "I've seen and noticed the freight company around town that Mister Chandler has and I can tell that he has worked diligently to make the business a success, but that in itself is not enough. You really have no collateral."

Both Lily and Ben's hopes started to dip.

The banker continued, "You do have a few dollars already and you both seem to come from good work stock ethics. Tell you what I'll do. I'm probably a little crazy for this, but you give me the buggy and I'll loan you the two hundred dollars. Interest will be at six percent and thirty dollar payments will be due every month, starting in sixty days."

Ben was first to acknowledge the agreement, "Thank you, Mister Harrison. We won't miss a payment, I assure you. And we can leave the buggy right now."

Stanley Harrison looked at Ben, "No, you'll need it to get home. Take your wife home and come back and leave it then. In the meantime, I'll have the papers drawn up to be signed and the money will be waiting for you when you get back."

On the ride home they were both relieved and happy to get the money. Even if they didn't get anything out of the buggy, they still came out ahead by about one hundred and fifty dollars. It would be enough to buy a wagon and another horse, if they were careful.

Ben brought Lily home, turned around and started back to the bank. "I won't be long," he promised.

Lily hurried inside. What to do first she wondered? Ah, the first thing is to write a quick note to her best friend, Anna Baker to let her know what was happening. She quickly finished that chore and then proceeded to set things out that needed to be packed even though they still did not know exactly when the next steamer would be leaving for Alaska. Then she thought, Oh my, she would have something interesting to put in her diary tonight.

Ben was back within three hours, a bit sore from riding the gray bareback. "I'm really not used to this," he groused good-naturedly.

Lily took it all in stride as she replied, "I always thought you wanted to be a cowboy. Now, you've got your chance."

"I think I've learned I'm not cut out for that. Anyway, I got the money right here in my pocket. He gave me a choice of a cashier's check or cash. I took the cash as I'd have to cash the check later anyhow."

The next day Ben set off for the docks in Tacoma to make arrangements for their passage. He found it would be cheaper to leave from Seattle and he was able to book passage on the steamer Al-ki for two people, one wagon and two horses. The ship was due to leave Seattle on July twenty-fifth. Just six days away. They didn't have much time to spare. He still had to buy another horse and wagon, plus fodder, food and other supplies. It would be close.

After he booked passage he stopped by the C & T Hauling and made arrangements with Einnar to ship everything to Seattle free. As a former manager he knew that he still had some clout and he was sure Vernon Tibbs would not object if he shipped his goods deadhead, or no charge. A goodly savings here, he realized.

With stubborn determination, they managed to arrive in Seattle on the twenty-fourth. Lily's long time friend, Angelina put them up for the night. Ben left the the gray and another tired brown work horse along with a newly purchased wagon filled with their belongings and supplies at the C & T warehouse overnight.

The next morning at dawn they were at dockside ready to load and board the Al-ki moored just south of the Schwabacher Wharf. The Al-ki was an old converted freighter that had been hurriedly adapted for the Alaska run. The docks were a mass of confusion as people tried to load possessions, animals, food and other goods. Fortunately Ben already knew the routine so he was able to get his papers all in order and load up with a minimum of problems. By nine in the morning both he and Lily were aboard and waiting for the other passengers to board with their property, but it wasn't until noon that the Al-ki finally got under way.

Lily looked over the crowded deck and estimated that there were about six hundred passengers on board, then turned and watched the skyline of Seattle slowly recede as they moved out into the waters of the Puget Sound. A slight tear came to her eye as she wondered what lay ahead. She was leaving good friends and customary daily routines. In the rushed confusion everything seemed so chaotic and confused. "Have we made the right move? What lies ahead?" she silently asked herself.

As the familiar slipped away, the chug, chug of the huge engines below deck brought calm and serenity to all on board. Everyone seemed to be occupied with the same thought. What was ahead and what will the future bring? Riches and luxury, or sadness and despair? Only the crew on board seemed to be relaxed as they proceeded to run the ship.

The quiet gradually ended as the passengers began to seek out their corners of privacy for the voyage ahead. Fortunately Ben anticipated that need and had booked a small cabin room that had two berths, but many of the others on board the crowded ship simply had to find a place, either above or below deck, that gave them some privacy and protection from the elements. The vessel had two restrooms, or heads as they are known by the crew. One on the main deck and one below deck. People had to stand in line to use the facilities and very soon the smell quickly became quite rank, especially below deck. Most of the animals were on the top deck, both fore and aft, and even though the waste was thrown overboard each day the odors permeated the entire ship. Most of the passengers tried to stay topside where the breeze would flush away the smell, but when the weather was inclement everyone suffered, except the crew who seemed to develop an immunity to it as they went about their daily tasks.

The Al-ki wound its way slowly up the inland passage along the coast of Canada's British Columbia. The islands to the west gave them protection from major storms coming off the Pacific Ocean, but it didn't stop the squalls completely. Often the passengers, animals and goods got thoroughly soaked from the heavy rains. Many travelers got seasick adding to the discomfort of everyone on board, especially those so afflicted.

Because of the large number of people, they had to eat in shifts. Some malingers tried to stay in the community kitchen and dining area as long as possible. It was warm and dry inside and there was always coffee available, but due to the circumstances they all were in, most seemed to cooperate well.

When the weather was clear many of the passengers would watch and listen to seals barking. Occasionally a whale could be seen, and on clear days, golden and bald eagles along with swarms of seagulls, competed for carrion in the waters and along the shoreline.

On a clear August third morning, the anxious group arrived off shore of Skagway and by ten in the morning they had gotten as close to the beach as possible. There were no docking facilities, so those passengers who were getting off had to wait for small boats or barges to come and take them and their luggage and equipment ashore. Rather than barge everything, some of the animals were pushed over board and had to swim to shore.

Afterwards the Al-ki backed off and headed up to the beach to Dyea about eight miles away. Most of those who remained on board were destined for Dyea as it was now known to be the cheapest way to get to the gold fields. It was low tide and once again small boats and barges had to shuttle the people and their belongings to shore, and again the animals were forced overboard and had to swim to land.

The beach was wide and muddy, and was now strewn with possessions that quickly became covered with sand, mud and grime. Lily could not believe her eyes and would have cried right here, but she realized that everyone was in the same situation. Everyone had to buck up and do what was necessary. There absolutely was no other choice.

People and beasts were covered in a mire of muck and mud. She boarded a small boat with a low draft, but it could not bring her all the way to shore, so she had to take off her shoes and wade the final forty feet. Once on shore, she knew they had to save their luggage, supplies and food before high tide came back in. She had no choice but to wade back in the wallow and start pulling their cargo to a higher spot on the beach above the high water mark.

Ben used ropes and pulleys, and with the help of others on board, had gotten their partially loaded wagon down off the ship and into the water. Then, aided by the two horses he had gotten off earlier, he managed to get a rope on the wagon tongue and was able to drag the wagon towards the beach line. Once above the high tide mark, they reloaded the items that Lily had rounded up. After tying everything down they proceeded up along the side of the Dyea River, also called the Taiya River by the local Indian population.

It was about two miles from the inlet, across a thinly wooded delta, to the trading post settlement of Dyea. Already the road had been become a mass of mud, partially filled in with rocks and trees by others who had proceeded them. The line of fortune seekers, wagons and horses, and other livestock continued to erode the poor trail.

More and more, Lily began to wonder what they had let themselves in for, especially when she began to see the settlement of Dyea come into view. "Ben, there is nowhere to stay," she remarked wide eyed as they approached the shanty town. "I only see about a half a dozen buildings, and those look more like cow sheds."

"Lily, don't worry. We'll be okay." He pointed ahead and tried to raise her spirits, "See all those tents being pitched."

"Yes, but we can't stay in those. They're someone else's, and beside that they all look like there are pitched in a sea of mud."

"Lily, we have the wagon, plus the tent we brought, and that will make our situation far better than these temporary squatters. Remember, they are here just for a night or two and then they will be moving on."

"And from the looks of this place, that's what we should be doing—moving on out of this hell hole!"

"Lily, take a good look. There must be five hundred people here at this moment. More will be coming this way everyday, and everyone of them has freight to be moved."

With their eyes opened in amazement, they rode down a crooked main street rutted and filled with mud. Dingy gray tents lined both sides of the route. Some of them already had signs out to sell their wares. There were two saloon tents, two restaurant tents. Others were advertising hardware and supplies, haircuts, guides and packing, gold pans and equipment, and even fortunes told.

Ben kept moving past the melee of scattered structures until he passed by four solid wood frame buildings. One of the weathered buildings had a sign that read 'Dyea Trading Post'. He continued past everything until he finally reached the edge of the small timber groves on the north end of the little valley.

Lily sat on the wagon in silence, too numb to speak about the conditions which they now found themselves in.

"Okay, we'll pull off in these trees. I know there's not many, and they're not very big, but they will provide some shelter for us and the horses. Lily, climb on down," he ordered, trying to bring her out of her despair. "Help me put up this tent. We need to get a fire going, and I have to feed and find water for ourselves and these horses."

Obediently Lily did as she was told and they finally got the ten by ten foot tent pitched and staked into solid ground. Ben found the small stove he had packed away and started a fire. After that he staked out and fed the two horses from his precious oats supply. Next he found a very narrow stream close by and soon brought back two five gallon cans of fresh water.

"Dammit Ben, you said it would be bad, but I sure didn't figure it would be as bad as this!" she said to him as she put the coffee pot on the now glowing red hot stove to brew.

"Hey, it will get a lot better," he said trying to be cheerful. "Tomorrow I'll start hauling freight for these new arrivals right off the beach. You'll see, in no time at all, we'll have a regular wood built house." Ben uttered the words, but right now, even he had a few doubts.

Lily glared at him, "It had better get a hell'va lot better!"

Although they didn't realize it at the time, they were lucky not to have it rain the day they landed. Nor did it rain the following day when he left Lily at the campsite that morning and headed for the beach with the two horses and wagon.

He returned after dark, tired, sore and dirty, but elated with the days events. "It's going to be a bonanza! I worked all day long. Didn't even have lunch, and I made twenty-five dollars! More than double what I made in Tacoma in a week!"

Lily was impressed, but definitely not overjoyed. She had been left alone all day in a depressing environment and she was still upset about it. Ben's return helped shed part of the anguish she was going though. "I just hope it continues to pay off. We have the banker's loan to pay for, and I don't know how long I can put up with these absolutely horrid living conditions!"

"Cheer up. I can see that this is going to be great! As long as there is gold in those hills, the money will continue to come in."

Ben was right with his prediction. There was plenty of freight to be hauled. All of the gold seekers were clamoring for packers, guides, horses, wagons, carts, sleds and dogs. Anything that could be used to haul their goods. He learned that the main trail to the Yukon gold territory was named Chilkoot and it extended north out of Dyea for about thirty miles. Various spots on the trail had names like Finigan's Point, Sheep Camp, and The Scales. The Scales being the final resting place before attempting the totally exhausting climb to the summit of the pass. He also learned from the operators of the trading post that the trail past The Scales was extremely difficult. The climb to the summit was almost straight up through a snow packed glacier.

The Northwest Mounted Police were stationed at the top of the pass and everyone had to show that they had two thousand pounds of provisions before they were allowed to enter the Canadian Yukon. All of these supplies had to be packed up the Chilkoot trail by the newcomers or by guides and packers hired for that purpose. At this point the trail was much too steep for animals, so it meant that many people had to make as many as eighteen to twenty-four trips up and down the mountain glacier to get all their supplies to the summit.

At the summit a ragged tent city had been erected while everyone waited for the Mounted Police to inspect their store of goods so they could get a pass to proceed. This large cache of provisions was to ensure the Canadian officials that the new comers would not perish in the remaining trek of some four hundred and twenty miles to Dawson and the gold fields. Yet often many people died in route as this was a dangerous journey over frozen lakes, snow fields, and in the spring, open lakes and very dangerous rivers and rapids that flowed northward towards Dawson.

Ben's freight business mushroomed! At the end of the first month he took the short trip over to Skagway and made arrangements to pay one hundred dollars back on the bank loan they had taken out in Tacoma. Thirty days later they had sent the final one hundred dollar payment plus interest. They never had to make the thirty dollar monthly payments originally agreed upon. A big financial weight was off their shoulders.

The little settlement of Dyea was growing almost faster than one could imagine. New wood frame buildings were now sprouting up at the rate of one every two weeks. A recent arrival, Mister Bailey had built a large hotel on the main muddy thoroughfare and almost across from him was a new trading post named Yukon Trading Company.

Many of the fortune hunters only had enough money to get to Dyea. Once there, they had to find work to earn money to buy supplies for their journey ahead. Thus it was easy for Ben to find carpenters, or at least men who called themselves carpenters, to build a small two room shanty with a lean-to on one end. They decided to build it at the north end of the settlement, but off the main Chilkoot trail so they could avoid some of the mud. Mud that was a certainty everywhere.

Lily and Ben were better off financially than they had ever been before. She had finally asserted herself and had gone to work for J.D. Bartlett who owned Bartlett Barber Shop and Saloon. It paid well, ten dollars per day serving drinks in the bar. Ben's business continued to grow and he bought six more horses from horse traders who brought in the animals to be sold as pack horses. Many of these creatures were so mean and ornery that it was almost impossible to get near them, but they were all quickly sold to the unsuspecting.

By early fall a dance hall, an open kitchen restaurant, two new saloons, and the Klondike Lodging House had been built. The lodging house advertising beds for twenty-five cents per night. It seemed almost over night that there were close to fifteen hundred people in Dyea. Things were happening fast. Almost too fast to cope with.

They were both making good money which they carefully hoarded in an old clay pot stashed in the attic space above the kitchen. However, it did require standing on a chair to reach the access opening to retrieve this hidden safe. Everything they owned was paid for outright, but riches of any kind always has its drawbacks, and Dyea's drawback was the climate and the setting.

Storms blew in almost continually from the coast and up the narrow valley, bringing rain, sleet, and often snow, as they came inland. The muddy streets never had time to dry out. The ruts made by the wheels of carts and wagons slowly drifted this way and that. Even as new structures were being built along the main street the road in front of the buildings remained about six to eight inches deep in mud. In the worst spots, unseen holes were filled with mud and muddy water about two feet deep. These were frequently the cause of stuck wagons, broken wagon wheels and axles. On some occasions horses and oxen would break their legs in one of the numerous holes and have to be put down.

In spite of these living conditions, the freight business remained good. "Lily, things are wonderful!" said Ben. "And I think we can do even better this coming year. There just doesn't seem to be any end of the people who are coming to get rich in the gold fields. Why just yesterday, I heard of an Indian named Charlie who hit it big at Dawson. Also a guy by the name of George Carmack, and another guy named Alex McDonald."

"I admit we're doing well, but others are learning how to handle freight too. I hear a lot while working in Bartlett's. There are more and more Indians working as packers now. Some of them with their wives and children working right along with them. From what I hear at the bar they are getting fifty cents a pound and up."

"You are right, but I've got the horses and wagons to handle more than they can carry, and a whole lot faster too." Ben paused, "Guess you have heard about all the hundreds of horses left to die on the trail."

Lily looked up from the ledger she was entering figures in. "Yes, I have, and if it is true, it's a shame." She glanced up from the table, "What's really going on up there?"

"People are beating them to death to force them up and over the rocks and trees. Most know that they can't get them up the trail past Scales, so they don't even feed them. It's no wonder they're dying. I'll tell you, it's a stinking awful mess in spots. The skeletons are so thick on some parts of the trail that they are just walked on. They're using bones for foot holds."

"I can't understand that type of cruelty."

"Well, this horse thing has given me an idea. I think I can get horses up on the other side of the summit by taking the White Pass Trail out of Skagway. It's a longer trail, and just now starting to be used. It's one hell'va lot less higher by about twelve hundred feet. Once over that, I can come back up the Chilkoot Trail from the other side and start packing supplies from the summit towards Dawson. I could haul down to Crater Lake, Happy Camp, or even to Long Lake beyond."

"Since you're talking this big expansion, I've got another idea. Mister Bartlett has offered to let me buy one half of his saloon business. What do you think?" She was careful not to mention that Jim Bartlett, or J.D. as he was known, seemed to have a crush on her.

"Right off the top of my head, I don't think you can go wrong." He stopped and reached for a chunk of cheese that she had sitting on the table by the ledger and cut off a piece. "What does he want for it? Any idea?"

"I'm not sure. He hasn't set a figure on it yet."

"Well, if it looks reasonable you should probably go for it, but we've got to be sure that sale is for the business and the property as well. We don't want to be caught like I was with Vernon Tibbs and find out it is for the profits only, or something similar."

Lily closed the ledger and pushed it back on the table, "You can be sure I won't let that happen."

As winter approached, Ben's freight hauling did slow down. The new comers were still coming into Dyea, but about half of them decided to wait until spring to attempt the long arduous trip over the mountains into the Yukon and the gold fields. There was still freight to be packed and hauled in as far up the Chilkoot trail as they could go with the horses, but now there were frequent snowfalls along the coast and in the mountains. Interestingly enough, there remained a few fortune hunters that actually preferred to travel in the winter when they could use their sleds and dogs to better advantage.

Ben used the slower time to increase his stock of good horses and to plan for the task of taking horses over the White Pass Trail in the spring. Meanwhile, Lily found herself busier than ever. More people in town for the winter meant more business for Bartlett's Saloon. They added a part time barmaid, and J.D. Bartlett made an arrangement with a professional gambler named Scotty Brown to set up a gaming table in one corner of the building. He rented the table space out for twenty-five dollars a week.

J.D. prided himself on his business acumen as he bragged, "Lily, you know, I'm a fool to sell you half of this saloon. Why this thing will probably make me a millionaire."

Lily smiled back coyly, "J.D., you're right, but this way we can both be millionaires! Why with your brains, and me running the show out front, how can we lose?"

He knew that there was some truth in what she said. "You asked me what I wanted for my half of the saloon business and I've been thinking about what would be fair for a pretty girl like you. How would you like to buy one half of it for fifteen hundred dollars?" He grinned knowingly, like the cat who has just caught a mouse.

She looked at the slightly over weight man standing behind the bar. The extra weight she knew was from his love of alcohol, probably beer. He definitely had the beginning of a pot belly. "Does that include one half of the building and the property?"

J.D., thought for a moment as he rubbed his chin, "Yes, but only the saloon portion. I'd keep the entire barber shop building and property next to the bar."

"And we'd split the saloon profits equally?"

"Yep," He stopped and touched the end of his short black mustache, "but we'd be splitting the costs equally too, you know."

"J.D., you've got a deal. I'll ask one of those legal brothers at Thompson and Associates over in Skagway to draw up the papers for your signature." She was in the driver's seat now, and she knew she had the deal she wanted.

"Lily honey, now you just go ahead and have them papers done up, and I'll sign them right off." J.D. did not even realize that he had been skillfully led into the deal by his desire for Lily.

That evening when Ben came in from work they discussed Lily's agreement with J.D. "You told him it was to be for one half of the property and building?" Ben questioned.

"I surely did."

"And you get one half of all the profits?"

"That's right, but like he says, I have to pay one half of the costs too. Guess that's only fair."

"And the price?"

"Fifteen hundred, which sounds awfully low, considering how much business the place in bringing in. I see the receipts each day, and it is around two hundred a day, sometimes up to three hundred. Plus there is another hundred coming in each month from Scotty Brown's gambling table."

Ben grinned from ear to ear, "Lily girl, I don't quite see how you can refuse."

Lily neglected to tell Ben that she thought J.D. had other things in mind, but she'd been able to cast off vultures before, and she was sure she could do it once again. The next day she made arrangements with Jack MacIntosh, who owned a small fishing boat, to take her to Skagway to have the papers drawn up before J.D. could change his mind.

The settlement at Skagway was over two times the size of Dyea. William Moore owned a good share of the property around the inlet and was in the process of supplying lumber from his sawmill for a new wharf he was having built. No longer would goods and people have to be dropped on the tide flats to flounder for themselves. There were still hundreds of tents scattered about, but there were now many wooden frame buildings that had been built as well. The Burkhard House hotel was almost finished on Broadway, and next to it was the legal offices of Thompson and Associates.

The two Thompson brothers were very busy. There was a long line of customers having papers made out for deed transfers, partnerships, sales, and loans. Lily waited her turn and soon they had a young male typist typing up the papers she required. After a careful review, she paid the bill of four dollars and returned to Dyea on the MacIntosh fishing boat. The total time, counting the wait in the office and a small meal in one of the numerous eateries on the main street, took five hours round trip.

That evening she and Ben painstakingly reread the document again. After both of them were satisfied, they retrieved their safe from the attic space and carefully counted out the fifteen hundred dollars. Lily made the entry in the ledger. The remainder was still a healthy nine hundred and twenty-two dollars. Enough left to get them though the coming winter and to enable Ben to buy feed for his small herd of horses.

The next morning Lily took the papers into Bartlett's Saloon. "I've got everything all written up just the way you wanted." She purposely stressed the words, 'the way you wanted'. "And I've got the money right here in the this money bag, all counted out to the penny," she added dropping the bag on the bar to emphasize her presentation.

"You don't waste any time, do you!" said J.D. as he reached into the envelope and took out the papers. "Let's see what you've got here." As he read the papers he murmured, "Yes, yes, hmm, yes."

Lily tried to help the process along, fearful that he might change his mind. "I made notes of everything you wanted. I'm sure I got it just the way you asked for it."

J.D. looked at her, then to the bag filled with money on the bar. "Yes, that seems to be just what we talked about." He looked at the bag again, "And there's fifteen hundred dollars in there?"

"Absolutely. Go ahead and count it."

He smiled wanly, "No Lily, I know I can trust you." He turned around and took his pen and a bottle of ink from out of a drawer in the back counter. "Now then, where do I sign this thing? Oh, I see right here at the bottom." Then he slowly wrote out, 'James D. Bartlett'.

One half of the Bartlett Saloon now belonged to Lily. She was twenty years old and it was the first tangible asset that she had ever owned in her life. She was now making more money in two or three months than her family made during an entire year. It may not have been in a business that they would have approved of, but it was hers and she knew she had been successful. Yes, she decided, it felt great!

The winter snows continued to fall heavily along the coastline and up in the mountains. Yet business remained good. The income from Lily's half of Bartlett's Saloon remained high, bringing into their savings an average of fifty dollars per month, which was over and above Lily's salary and tips. Ben's income had dipped slightly, but he used the time to repair tack, other equipment, and to fatten up his horses for the hard spring labors ahead. He still planned on taking part of his horse herd to the other side of Chilkoot Pass in the spring by way of the lower elevation and longer White Pass trail out of Skagway.

When Ben wasn't busy with his freight or his animals, he often spent time with some of the other business people. Among these were tent store owners, packers, hardware merchants and guides discussing business. He learned through others in town that some Skagway promoters were proposing to build a railroad over the lower pass clear into Dawson. If it came to pass, it could put him out of business, but for the present, he was not particularly worried. It probably would never happen. Yet again, it was something to keep in mind.

The overcast and darkness of the season wore on everyone. Things were stymied. People were anxious to get moving towards the gold fields to make their fortunes. Many of the men left their families to make the run to Dawson in the winter time anyway and planned to send for their families later. A few took their wives and children up and over Chilkoot Pass in the deep snow with temperatures that dropped down to fifty below zero. A good many of these travelers died from hypothermia and accidents in the treacherous mountains. Under these trying circumstances many of those who impatiently remained in Dyea for better traveling conditions became quiet, sullen and moody.

Lily noticed that even Ben was not as upbeat as he had been in the past. He was becoming broody and a bit short tempered. She knew that spring was just around the corner and she was sure he would be his same old optimistic self once the weather improved. After all, they were still making money even in the middle of the wintertime, but she did not fully understand that working out in the blowing rain and snow day after day gets on one's nerves. It was a very miserable existence, trying to work, trying to stay dry, and trying to stay warm.

Christmas came on another cold and wet dreary day, and even though they were in a warm house, unlike those who were still living in tents, there was not much to celebrate. Lily was still working every day, so she really hadn't done much to enhance the holiday season. At the last moment, she hung a few bright bows on the walls, and one on the front door, but she had no time for making Christmas pastries.

Lily suggested that they both stay home Christmas day. She pointed out that this could be a day where they just sat back and relaxed. Maybe talk a little and take it easy. She said this in hopes of having Ben open up about what seemed to be bothering him.

"Can't really do that," said Ben. "Have to make sure the horses are tended to."

She tried to meet him half way. "That won't take more than a couple of hours. We can still enjoy what's left."

He sat in his chair, not saying anything.

"Ben look, I know something's troubling you. What is it?"

"Dammit Lily, I don't really know. I guess it's the weather. The talk of a railroad being built." He looked up at her, "That'd just about kill my business you know. And there's more competition now. I just know that this next year isn't going to be so good. I can feel it in my bones. Plus it's hard on me not seeing you around home anymore. You're always off at work. It's just all these things, all rolled up into one."

"Well, we could sell off everything and go back down to the states. We've done pretty well, and we could find something to do in Seattle or Tacoma, I'm sure."

"Lily, I just don't know. There are guys making their fortunes in gold up in the Yukon, and I can feel our position slipping away. I really don't know what the answer is."

"You've said before that by getting your horses up on the other side of Chilkoot Pass you can get a lot more business. That ought to help."

"You forget, that if that damn railroad does go in, there'll be no more need for any horses, packers, guides, or anything. I'll be out of business. Remember when the railroad extended into Seattle. It was all we could do to hold our heads above water at C & T Hauling. I just don't know what to do."

Lily turned and cut off a slice of white cake she had bought from one of the ladies who worked out of a tent store, "Here, at least enjoy a piece of this cake." She felt that in time things would work out. She reasoned that as soon as the days start to clear and the snow starts to melt he would feel better about the situation.

On the ninth of January Lily turned twenty one. There was no party, no fanfare of any type. Nor did she mention it to anyone. It was merely another date in time. In Ben's temperamental state he had forgotten it as well, so Lily did not remind him. It would have only added to his worries. She had been working at Bartlett's for close to four months and age was not a consideration in a bar, or anywhere else in Alaska. If you could do the job, it was yours.

The bad weather and the long dark days of the new year only brought more gloom and discomfort to those confined at Dyea. Ben still remained moody, and if anything a bit more sullen and withdrawn. The oppressive situation effected everyone. Fights and arguments broke out among strangers, good friends and families. Lily noticed it daily at Bartlett's Saloon where J.D. had to step in and break up arguments before they escalated into a swinging free for all, with knives, clubs, boots and plain old bloody fist fights.

By the end of March the days began to lengthen and the bad weather eased up. It didn't stop, but every day or so, you could see the sun trying to poke though the storm clouds. Spirits were slowly improving as the fortune hunters knew they would soon be on the way up the Chilkoot Trail and on to Dawson City in the Yukon.

Even though the freight business was slowly starting to pick up for Ben, he often sat at the table in the evenings and grumbled about, "that damn railroad they were building out of Skagway". The thought of it grew on him more and more. "Lily, I only see one solution."

She continued pouring rinse water from the tea kettle over the dishes she had been washing. "And what is that?"

"I've made up my mind. I'm going to sell off the freight business, the horses, hay, packs, harnesses, the whole damn thing."

"And then what?"

"I plan on keeping the six best horses and packs. We've got the attic safe, and there's plenty of money in that to hold you for any emergency that may come up. I can get enough out of the other animals, wagons, and outbuildings to cover my costs during the time I'm up in Dawson. It will all work out."

"Up in Dawson!" Lily exclaimed.

"Yes, up in Dawson. I'm going to get us some of that gold too! The freight business will soon be lost to that damn railroad anyway."

"You can't be serious!"

"I'm dead serious."

"Oh Ben, I don't know. I've seen too many families broken up by men who have gone off to their deaths in those horrible mountains. These kinda things bring on divorce and break up families."

"Look, nobody knows that Chilkoot trail better than me. I know what the risks are. I've been up and down that damn thing hundreds of times."

"But you've only been up to The Scales. Not the remaining four hundred miles on into Dawson. How can you possibly think of such a thing?" Lily paused, then threatened, "If you go, I'll get a divorce. I'm not gonna to be left a widow, always wondering what happened to my husband." She was saying anything that came to her mind, trying to make Ben come to his senses.

Ben's jaw firmed, "There will be no divorce. I'm not giving you one, now or ever. You're my wife, and there's never been a divorce in the Chandler family, and we're not going to start now." The veins on the side of his neck began to enlarge. "You're going to wait right here for me until I get our gold, then I'll come on back for you and we can go where ever you want to go. South America, New York, anywhere at all."

"I don't like this one damn bit!"

"Well, you're going to wait right here, and if you're not here when I come back, I'll be coming after you wherever you are! And that's it!" Ben said as he got up and went out the door, slamming it loudly behind him.

Lily sat on the edge of her chair, not moving. Stunned by what was happening. Numbed by the events, and unable to even cry. She sat on the chair for two hours, then got up and went to bed, but she did not sleep. She tossed and turned trying to sort out what was happening in her life. She heard Ben come in much later, heard the sound of his boots on the wooden kitchen floor, heard the faint sound of whiskey being poured in a cup and water being added.

The demand for anything to haul freight was still high and the next morning Ben quickly sold off his wagons, extra horses and tack. He packed his remaining six horses with the two thousand pounds of staples required by the Canadian authorities. Three of the horses he packed with food which included flour, oatmeal, sugar, salt, baking powder, dried fruit, yeast cakes, dried potatoes, and soda. Another horse he loaded down with a small cooking stove, pots, pans and utensils, oats for the horses, and extra tack. On the remaining two horses he packed hay for the animals. All six of the animals were covered by canvas that could also be used for shelter. By late afternoon it was drizzling lightly as he left for the Yukon Territory.

Even for a seasoned trail hand the four hundred miles trip posed all sorts of problems other just than the extreme severe weather. Many experienced men died from exposure and accidents, but for the hundreds of clerks, yard hands, office workers, and other novice fortune hunters, the snow storms and the cold took an extremely heavy toll. Some froze and died on the way, many just disappeared, never to be seen again. Others fell to their deaths from the high mountains. Some drowned in the waters of Crater Lake, Long Lake and Bennett Lake on the north eastern side of the Chilkoot and White Pass trails. Still others perished in the rapids of the Yukon River that flowed through those lakes towards Dawson.

Suddenly Lily had to cope with being alone and protect herself. She bought more firewood from those trying to make grub stake money. Every morning before going to work she began to cut up some of the wood and stacked it under the lean-to to dry out. She bought her food from the stores and tent vendors. In the past Ben had often brought home food in exchange for hauling freight, but all that was behind her now. She had to make her own way.

Being at work helped, but did not completely erase the anger and frustration she felt at Ben for leaving her. She began to confide with her business partner, J.D. Bartlett, not realizing he was relishing every thing that had happened to her.

It was the very reason he had sold her part of the saloon business, hoping to become a confidant and that he could step into her life.

"These things happen, Lily. Ben's got gold fever. That's just the way it is. Some of us are more level headed, so we don't get caught up in it. Just remember you have a friend in me. I'll help you get through this. Things will get better, I promise," said J.D. as he put his arm around her shoulder.

"J.D., you've been a good friend, and thank you for listening to me. I don't mean to trouble you with my problems."

"Now Lily, you're no trouble. After all we're business partners. Part of the same mold so to speak."

"Thanks J.D., I won't let you down."

"I'm sure you won't Lily, I'm sure you won't," he said, patting her on the shoulder.

That afternoon Lily begged off from work early. "J.D., I've just got to get out. Got to get some fresh air."

"Now you just go ahead. Ain't any heads of hair to be cut in the evening anyway, so me and Scotty can handle the bar."

Grateful to get out of the smoke filled saloon, she wandered past the other shops and tent stores thinking about what was happening. She glimpsed the new wharf being built at Dyea without it really registering in her mind. She just knew it was taking place, but she really did not focus on it. She looked over the tops of the mountains of supplies sitting just above the high tide mark on the beach, past the tents hastily erected, past the scores of people waiting to move on. She didn't even notice the pungent odor of manure in the muddy roadway or the rank smells of the out houses and latrines. None of it was really registering. She was in her own confused world.

At the end of the muddy street, she turned and began to make her way back past the stores and tents, being careful to try and walk where she would not step in the manure or in a mud hole. As she walked by the Bailey Hotel she noticed a sign in the window, "Mail Pick Up this Friday". She stopped to stare at the sign. "Mail," she said aloud. "Mail, that's what I'll do. I'll write to Anna. Maybe even ask her to come up here."

Now with a purpose in mind, she hurried home to write to her best friend. She wrote that Ben had left and explained how lost she was without him. Then she included an invitation for her to come to Dyea for a visit for a month or so until things straightened themselves out, offering to pay Anna's fare and saying they could share her house. She carefully blotted the letter, folded it up and took it down to Bailey's Hotel to be mailed out the next day.

Work was a big release. It kept her mind occupied. J.D. frequently came over into the saloon to check on her when he was not cutting hair next door. Most of the time she was able to cope with her loss by keeping busy, as there was beer and whiskey to inventory and order from one of the two trading posts. In addition there were always floors to sweep, counters to be wiped down, windows to be cleaned, and glasses to be washed and put away.

Late one evening after closing time as J.D. came in from the barber shop next door, he said, "Hey Lily, come sit down and relax, I'll pour us each a beer."

"Thanks J.D. I shouldn't, but I will take that drink. I think I could use it about now."

"How you getting along? Do you have enough food, money? You doing okay?" asked J.D. as he pretended to have her best interest at heart.

"I'm doing okay."

"You know I'm here to help. Even if you just need someone to lean on, I'm here."

"I know that J.D.," said Lily as she paused to take a drink. "You've been a great help. I really don't think I could have gotten along this far without your help. You've been a true friend." Lily stood up, "I've got to go now. It's been a long trying day,"

"Do you want me to walk you home? There's a lot of trouble makers out there, and I don't want to see anything happen to you, partner," he asked.

"I think I'd like that. I'd feel a bit safer that's for sure. Thanks J.D."

He walked her home, being every inch the gentleman. Not crossing the line for a moment as he was sure that she would be caught up in his web very slowly. He could sense that his time would come if he was very careful and patient.

Gradually, at J.D.'s invitation, she began to linger at the saloon for a while before coming home at nights to an empty house with its worries and boredom. It became the norm for the both of them to have a couple of drinks each evening after closing. All the time J.D. remained courteous and helpful. Offering money, and that shoulder to cry on. As the weeks passed Lily began to look forward to their evenings together, and a little drink to relax with. Occasionally J.D. would add just a spoonful of whisky to her beer, 'to flavor it', as he put it.

Each morning she would wake up, and look at the calendar on the wall. It was now March second. Ben had been gone for one full month. She thought about it, and came to the conclusion that her only friend in Dyea was J.D. She had no others. Then thinking of friends, she thought about the letter she had written to Anna Baker some three weeks past. In the loneliness of the little house, she wondered if Anna had received her letter, and if she had written back. She decided that she'd check the mail drop at Bailey's Hotel when she went to buy some meat and bread from the tent vendors this morning.

Nearing the center of Dyea, she noticed a few new boardwalks had been built in front of the stores to keep the people out of the mud. It was a long needed and welcome addition. She recalled hearing from one of the barroom patrons that someone had even opened a church in town, and thought at that time, what a waste of effort! Too late to save any souls in this hell hole. As she walked past shops with signs hawking their wares, she realized that this place was bustling and still growing. Maybe there could be a future here.

She walked into the Bailey's Hotel and asked the clerk behind the counter if she had any mail. He turned around to sort through a box of mail behind him. "Let's see. Lily Chandler, Lily Chandler," he repeated to himself as he sorted through the mail that was kept in an old wooden apple box crate. "Ah, yes. Here we go. One letter from an Anna Baker," said the clerk as he turned and handed it to her.

Lily was thrilled to get Anna's letter, and quickly opened it and began to read. Anna was coming! And should arrive on the steamship City of Seattle on March fourth. She suddenly comprehended. My God! That's only two days away!

She rushed excitedly from the building. I've got to get home and make sure I've got clean bedding on the bed. And food, what food do I have? I've got to make a list of what we might need. These thoughts and others rushed though her mind as she hurried back home after buying fresh eggs, meat and bread from the tent vendors. Back at her cabin, she put the eggs and meat in the cooler built between the kitchen and the outside lean-to for firewood. Next she set about trying to clean the place up. Picking up a broom she began to sweep, then abruptly realized that the dust and dirt were extremely heavy because she had neglected her housework. She went to the water bucket, carefully filled a small bottle with water, added the sprinkler cap pierced with holes, and began to lightly sprinkle the floor. After that, she began sweeping again and the dust remained at a tolerable level. Dishes that had been also neglected were now washed and put away. She looked at the clock on the bed stand. Windows and curtains that needed washing would have to wait until later. Right now she had to leave for work. I'm sure that Anna will understand, she thought to herself.

Essie, the part time barmaid, was behind the counter serving beer to two sourdoughs. Lily recognized the pair of regulars as hot air talkers, not doers. Both were inclined to dispense their vast knowledge of the Yukon to any new comer who might buy them drinks.

"Morning Essie," said Lily as she walked past the two men at the bar. "Where's J.D.?"

"He's next door, finally trying to clean the place up a bit."

"Thanks," said Lily as she walked through the opening and entered the barber shop.

J.D. had a broom and dust pan in hand and was sweeping up hair from around a chair on an elevated platform. Then he began to sweep around the base of the platform, filling the dustpan again and again with every color of hair one could imagine. All of it littered the wooden floor along with caked mud and dirt from the boots of the customers. It was evident that he had not swept out for quite a period of time. Perhaps never!

"Morning J.D.," said Lily with a big smile. "Looks like you may need a shovel rather than that little broom. I never realized how dirty this place was over here. Why I keep the saloon cleaner than this!"

J.D. straightened up from his task. "Now what brings you over into man's domain with a great big smile on your face? I can tell something is on your mind."

"You're right. I do have something on my mind. I need to take tomorrow off." She had learned that often when speaking with men it was best to get straight to the point.

"Lily, you know that you can have it off. Take any time you need," he said in a quiet way. "What's going on? Anything I can help with?"

"No. It's just that my best friend, Anna Baker, is coming in tomorrow on the City of Seattle to spend a few weeks with me."

"That sounds good," said J.D., but actually he was a bit concerned that this meeting with her friend may muddle up the ground work that he had been laying for Lily. "You just do what you have to do. Me and Scotty will handle things, and I can call Essie in again to help out. It will all work out fine," he said, working to salvage his plan.

The City of Seattle came in at low tide the next afternoon and prepared to off load its cargo and passengers. Lily was grateful for an overcast day and watched the proceedings from the beach. Most of the passengers were ferried to shore in small flat bottom wooden boats that had been specially constructed in Dyea. She craned her neck to see above the crowd of people. Then she saw a woman wearing a pink rose colored hat with a white plume feather in it. She walked perfectly straight, almost with a regal bearing, it had to be Anna. She would recognize that walk anywhere.

"Anna, Anna," she yelled over the heads of those still off loading. "Over here."

Anna Baker heard her call, looked and waved back before picking up her two suitcases, and began making her way through the crowd. In a few moments they were in each others arms and hugging.

"Oh Anna, it's so good to see you! I can't believe you're really here!"

"I'm glad to be here, I think," replied Anna as she looked at her surroundings. "What kind of a hole is this anyway?"

"It's not as bad as it looks at first." Lily reached for one of her suit cases. "Here, let me take one of these. Just try to keep out of the muck"

"My God! This looks like total confusion in a swamp!"

"Just follow me. I'll help you. To begin with, all the freight and the animals have to come ashore while the tide is out. Then everyone has to rush to get their belongs out of the mud and above the high tide mark or lose it. All these new comers will be scrambling to find a place to pitch their tents, or otherwise find shelter until they can get organized and get on the move again. Some will pitch their tents right next to their supplies, in the mud, around stumps still poking up, any place they can find."

Anna replied, "I'm just stunned! I've never seen anything like this!"

They began slowly walking and picking their way into the main part of Dyea with its rough weathered store fronts and tent vendors scattered throughout. "Let's get up here on the boardwalk, but be careful. The wet spots can be slick as a greased pig's back."

"Do I really see goats with packs on them?"

Lily looked out into the muddy road. "Yes, you do. You'll see horses, mules, even oxen with packs on them." She kicked at a dog laying down blocking the walkway. "Even dogs with packs, and there are sled dogs pulling sleds with packs on them as well. You'll see everything here."

"And I came up here! What was I thinking? I had no idea it was," she hesitated not wanting to have everyone hear what she was saying, then spoke quietly, "utterly filthy."

"It's not so bad at my house, but again it's not much either. A two room cabin, with an out house in back. There is a lot less mud though."

By the time they reached the cabin, both of the women had sore arms from carrying the heavy suit cases. Lily opened the door and scooted the suit case she had been lugging inside. "What have you got in here, bricks?"

Anna dropped her suit case to the floor with a loud thud. "Only what I need. Nothing more." She let her purse with its long shoulder strap drop slowly to the floor, then sat down on one of the two chairs. "With only two chairs, I take it you don't entertain much."

"No, not much, just occasionally the mayor and a few of his close friends," she said facetiously. "Seriously, I'm so glad you came. I just got your letter two days ago and found out you were on the way. I thought you'd write back first, 'cause I wanted to send you the money for the passage."

Anna stretched out her legs, "Let me explain. I got your letter on the nineteenth and thought how thrilling it would be to come up here. So I got hold of a friend of mine, actually a cousin of my dad's named Clarence Emery in Seattle, and asked him about getting a ticket to come up here. He called back the next day and said he could book me on the City of Seattle headed for Skagway and Dyea on February the twenty-fourth. There was no time to write you and wait for your reply, so I just sent you the one letter on the same day I booked the ticket, and crossed my fingers and hoped it would get to you before I arrived." She took a deep breath, "and I'm so glad you got that letter and was there to meet me. I would have been absolutely lost and terrified if you hadn't been there."

"Wow!" said Lily as she too marveled that she received the letter before Anna arrived. "Somebody up there likes you, that's for sure." Then she recalled the fare, "What did the ticket cost?"

"Clarence said he got a deal. Since it was round trip, and prepaid, the price was one hundred and seventy-five dollars. I don't know if that's out of line or what, but I had to make up my mind quickly, so I took it."

"I think you got a good deal, but even I don't know for sure. I've heard of fares running from thirty dollars up to three hundred dollars, and I don't think any of those were round trip, so I think your friend did okay by you. But I really don't care what it cost. I'm just so happy to see you, to have someone to talk to."

Lily added some wood to the kitchen stove. "Let's have something to eat. I'm sure you're probably hungry after your voyage up here to this wonderland." After they ate, the two young women talked the evening away as they unpacked the suit cases, rehashed old events and began catching up on new ones. It was close to one in the morning when they finally climbed in the iron frame double bed and went to sleep.

Another Pacific coast storm blew in during the night bringing in rain, sleet and light flurries of snow. When Lily got up she could see the snow was not sticking at the lower elevations, but she knew that the mountains and the passes were catching it, and worried about how Ben might be faring.

Anna sat up on the edge of the bed and looked out at the blowing wind and rain. "Absolutely wonderful climate you have here."

The smell of bacon frying drifted across the room. Lily glanced at her friend, "Coffee is on, How do you like your eggs?"

While they leisurely ate their breakfast, Lily said, "I've got to be at work at eleven. Probably get back about ten tonight after everything is done and put away. Why don't you just relax today. The weather will probably be a bit too miserable anyway to go out. But if you do go out, you know where the main street is, and Bartlett's Saloon is right near Bailey's Hotel. If you should happen to come by, I'll introduce you to my friend J.D."

"Yes, I remember seeing the saloon when I came in, but I'm not sure I should even go near the place. It looks so bad."

"All bars and saloons look bad, but I've made good money from Bartlett's, almost as much as Ben was making in the freight business. I guess I told you I own half of Bartlett's bar."

"Yes, you mentioned it in your letter to me, that's one of the reasons I came up here. I was curious to see it." Anna pushed her plate back and reached for her cup of coffee, "Don't be concerned about the cleanup here. I'll heat up some water and do the dishes. After all, like you say, it looks too miserable to go out anyway. You go on to work. I'll meet your friend J.D. later."

"Okay, I'll head off, but first I've got to pay you." Lily got up and moved her chair under the attic access opening, then stood on the chair and reached up into the attic and retrieved the clay pot. "This is our attic safe, as Ben called it." She sat the pot on the table, reached in and then began to count out one hundred and seventy-five dollars. "This is what I owe you for the fare."

"Certainly not the whole amount," Anna protested lightly.

"Yes, the whole amount. That's what I promised to do when I wrote you and that's the way it shall be." Then she dropped the remaining money back into the pot along with the partnership papers she had signed for the bar. She stepped up on the chair again, and returned the 'safe' to its original position and eased the attic board back in place.

"Don't you believe in banks?" asked Anna wide eyed.

"Not too much up here. Over in Skagway, there are a couple of places that called themselves banks. Sometimes people who put their money in them never see it again. So around here if you have any money, you don't show it. You just plead poverty, unless you know someone very, very well and feel you can really trust them."

"I see."

After Lily went off to work the weather improved so Anna decided to explore the settlement. She tried to stay out of the mud as she walked past the shabby buildings and tattered tents occupied with families, goods and animals. Wide eyed she watched in amazement at the comings and goings of the fortune hunters as they began making arrangements to continue their trek to the gold fields. She saw con men at work taking the new comers' money by gambling, and in some cases out and out theft. There appeared to be no law enforcement anywhere. She did notice there were a few semi honest business people who seemed to have a few scruples and would try to deal somewhat fairly. But, by and large, it was every person for themselves.

Anna turned around and walked back up the muddy street towards Bartlett's Saloon. Approaching the windowed door, she mustered up her courage and entered the dingy, smoke filled establishment. Lily was serving beer to a group of men seated at table in the back of the building next to the stove.

Lily looked up and saw Anna looking somewhat hesitant. "Anna, come on in. Let me show you around. Let me introduce you to the boys here." She pointed towards the corner. "That's Scotty Brown over there at the poker table." Scotty looked at Anna and nodded slightly and went back to his game. "The boys at the table are trying to stay warm and dry," she said more quietly. "Come on, I'll take you into the barber shop to meet J.D."

"Should I be going in there?" Anna questioned.

"It's okay. Remember, this is Alaska. Most anything goes up here."

They walked into the attached barber shop, and Anna looked at the stocky man giving a shave to a middle aged man with very muddy boots and pants. Dried mud and hair was thoroughly mixed on the floor around the elevated chair. A mirror hung on the back wall, and beside it was a partial glass of beer sitting on a shelf. The initials 'J.D.' were on the glass.

"J.D., this is my friend Anna that I told you was coming up for a visit."

J.D. stopped shaving his customer, and with the razor still in his hand, turned towards Anna. "Nice to meet you. Lily has told me that you have been friends for a long time." He gave Anna a careful look from top to bottom. "Hope to see you around town."

His eyes betrayed him Anna thought. He seemed like a lecher. "Yes, well I can't stay here very long. I'll have to get back to Seattle soon. Nice to meet you too," she said trying to be polite.

Lily continued to work and Anna left to continue looking at the sights in Dyea. Often it was after midnight when Lily would get home and Anna would be already in bed. Then she would tip toe in, light the kerosene lamp and turn it down low and prepare for bed. Sometimes Anna would wake up and they'd talk a bit before Lily came to bed, still reeking of strong cigarette and cigar smoke, and having liquor on her breath.

One day when Anna felt Lily was in a very good mood, she remarked about it. "You've got a tough job Lily. All the smoke in that place makes you smell like a chimney. I know you try to wash it all away, but I'll bet that after a while, you don't even smell it." She was attempting to approach the subject tactfully.

"I'm sure you're right. I have pretty much gotten used to it, so I don't hardy smell it anymore unless it gets really bad. Thanks for mentioning it. Guess I'll try to be more aware of it."

"And I worry about you. It seems to me that you're having a few more drinks than you should with J.D. after work."

"Oh that. It just helps me unwind. J.D. and I relax and go over things that we need to do, or whatever. There's no problem there."

"I think J.D.'s already got a problem. The few times I've been in the bar he seemed to have a beer in his hands. He's already got a beer belly. How much of the hard stuff does he drink after you close up?'

"You know, I haven't really noticed. Really both of us just use it to relax a bit."

"Well, I'd watch him closely. He seems to have his eyes on the women, if you get my drift."

"J.D.? You're kidding! We're just good friends, and business partners."

"It's just that I'd be careful."

"Oh Anna, you read too much into everything. Even if there was anything, I can handle it. You're not aware, but when I worked in Seattle at the Rochester House, there was this guy named Ron Appleton who got a little possessive, and I was able to handle him. You've got to realize that working in a bar, a girl soon learns how to handle the guys who step out of line."

"Just the same, I'd be careful."

The time flew quickly by, and after two weeks, Anna decided that she must return to Washington. The City of Seattle was due back in Dyea on the twenty-fourth of March and Anna had to catch that particular return trip or wait another full month before leaving.

Lily took the day off to see Anna leave. J.D. was quite relieved to hear she was leaving. Now he could concentrate on the task at hand. Mainly, Lily.

The two women lugged Anna's two heavy bags down to the beach and began the wait for the City of Seattle to appear. About four in the afternoon at low tide, the steamer dropped anchor off shore as the new wharf was still not finished. Now the procession of goods and people began moving on shore in earnest. Anna waited a while for a number of people to get off before trying to get in line for a ride back out to the vessel on one of the flat bottom barges.

Tearfully the two exchanges hugs. "Thank you so very much for coming. Thank you for everything. You've helped me more than you'll ever know. I promise I'll write, and I'll come visit you in Tacoma," said Lily.

"Please do. I'll wait for your letters, and please be careful here," warned Anna as she pushed her luggage up a narrow gang plank onto the out going barge.

"I will," she promised as she called from the beach and strained to watch for her friend as the small barge pushed off from the muddy and smelly tide flats. She saw Anna climb onto the main deck of the steamer and remained looking until the vessel pulled anchor and began to leave the small harbor. She almost wished that she had gone with Anna, but she knew she had obligations in Dyea.

She turned and walked up the beach towards home, but then detoured and went into Bartlett's. She walked in and went up to the bar and sat down. "Essie, bring me a whiskey. I think I need a drink right about now."

Within two days, it was back to the same old boring grind with J.D. and Lily starting to drink more and more after business hours. She missed Ben, she missed Anna, and J.D. began to fill that void. And he sympathized with her and her concerns. Eventually these late evenings led to drunken late nights of wild tales, jokes, and ultimately, a show of deep concern for each other.

It was during one of these late nights, that J.D. convinced Lily to stay the night. It really did not take much convincing as she was in no condition to walk home. When she woke the next morning, she was in J.D.'s bed. Although her head still hurt and her mind was foggy, she knew they had made love, and it didn't matter to Lily. J.D. was here. He had protected her and looked after her. He was her friend when everyone else had deserted her. That night after work, she made no pretense of going to her house. She had her late night drinks and retired to J.D.'s small bedroom. He was comfortable, and he would care for her.

It began to snow again on the first of April and the high mountains got another five to six feet of the heavy wet snow while the area around Dyea only received a modest six inches. As the reports came in from the Chilkoot Trail Lily silently wondered if Ben had been trapped on the far side of the summit in the heavy snow.

A couple of days later she was talking with Scotty in the bar when a man burst in through the door and yelled, "We need help on the trail! There's been a big avalanche, and about seventy people have been buried!"

The two sourdoughs at the bar set their beers down as one asked, "Where 'bouts on the trail?"

The newcomer gathered his breath, "Just beyond Sheep Camp. We need any help you can give us, man power, shovels, food, blankets. We're loading out a couple of wagons right now!"

Although she had never been up the trail Lily knew that the area just beyond Sheep's Camp had a reputation for many deaths, accidents, loss of animals and equipment. Beyond Sheep's Camp the trail led to The Scales, and from there the final hike to the summit. She called to the man in the doorway, "Wait, we've got extra bedding." Quickly she turned and ran to a back storage room and returned with an armload of old frayed blankets, knowing that they might help keep someone from freezing to death.

The two men at the bar ran outside to join the rescue train and Lily followed them out the door and tossed the blankets up to a woman trying to stack supplies in the wagon. Then very quickly, they were gone as they rushed up the muddy trail to search for survivors. Lily found out later that approximately sixty people had perished in avalanches that day. The final tally would never be known.

After that the days moved by slowly. April ended in a haze and May started. There were no letters or any information on Ben and Lily began to think that something had happened to him and that he was never coming back. But there remained a sinister feeling, that if he did come back, he would come looking for her. She remembered telling Anna she would write, but hadn't got around to it, plus she used the excuse, that Anna hadn't written to her either. Not even to thank her for paying her way up to Dyea and back. The alcohol was beginning to twist her outlook on life.

One late night, when Lily was thinking clear, she was starting to become aware that J.D. was drinking much more than he had in the past and that he was becoming more demanding and much less attentive to her. That night after work she poured each of them a double shot of whiskey and sat down on a bar stool, then asked, "J.D., do you think we are drinking too much?"

"What do you mean?" he stammered.

"Sometimes I get the feeling that perhaps we're drinking too much of this stuff."

"Where in the hell did you ever get a crazy idea like that? It helps, or rather keeps us from going crazy in this place. Dammit Lily, I don't know where you get such goofy ideas."

"You're not worried about it?"

"No, not a bit."

"J.D., I am. Maybe I need to get away for a while. Perhaps go down and see Anna for a week or so."

"What?" J.D. felt threatened and looked straight into Lily's face. "You're not going anywhere. You're my woman and we've got a business here to run."

Lily began to feel a little hot under the collar. "I'm nobody's woman, and certainly not yours!"

She tried to duck as his fist came around and hit her along the side of her face knocking her off the bar stool. "Don't ever talk to me like that! I own you lock, stock and barrel! Why do you think I sold you half of this business so cheap? It's because I bought you, and don't ever forget it!"

Lily's jaw pained and she was stunned. She sat on the floor crying. Anna was right all along. All J.D. really wanted was her. He was not the benefactor that he had pretended to be.

He walked around the end of the bar and glared down at her. "Get off your butt and get out of my sight, and don't ever talk to me like that again!"

She quit crying and got up and went to the bedroom and fell into bed, lost, hurt and bewildered. She lay there with her aching jaw throbbing and could hear J.D. swearing out in the other room behind the bar. What had she gotten herself into and how could she get out of it, she wondered? And what will he be like when he comes to bed later?

Long after midnight J.D. finally came into the bedroom and fell on the bed. He passed out and lay there the rest of the night with his clothes on, much to Lily's relief.

Late the next morning she eased out of the bed, careful not to wake J.D. from his drunken slumber. She went into the saloon and looked at her image in the mirror behind the bar. The side of her face was badly bruised and she could see swelling around her right eye. What to do right now was the question. She walked to the end of the counter and got a clean bar rag and soaked it in a cold water bucket and held it up to the side of her face. It hurt to the touch, but she could move her mouth and knew nothing was broken. She sat on a bar stool trying to gather her wits about her as she held the wet towel against her face.

She began to review her options. If she ran off to her house, she was sure J.D. would come and drag her back to the bar. And what about Ben? Was he even alive anymore? He had a deep sense of righteousness, and if he did come back and found out what had happened, no telling what he was capable of doing when he got really mad. Could she leave? If so, where would she go? Could she book passage and leave this forsaken place? This would probably not work, because if J.D. got suspicious he could find out by checking ticket sources along the waterfront. She needed help to leave she decided, and the only confidant she had left was Anna.

She had seen too many women beaten by drunken men and realized she was in a trap and had to get out of it as soon as possible. Right at that moment she decided to write to Anna and ask her to buy a ticket out of Dyea and mail it to her, but in the meantime she would have to be careful and not tip her hand to J.D. She'd have to mask her trips to Bailey's tiny post office when making the liquor pickups at the two trading posts.

She dabbed the wet cloth around the bruised area, then proceeded to act on her plan. She decided she would play the role of a meek submissive woman. Carefully she combed out her hair and applied what make up she had to try and cover up the bruise as best she could, then she went into action. She thoroughly swept out the bar room and proceeded to clean everything just as clean as possible. She wanted to leave no excuse for J.D. to be provoked. She inventoried the beer and liquor behind the bar and made out an order just like every normal day.

A rattle at the front door startled her and then she saw it was Scotty Brown who ran the poker table. Already she was becoming jumpy, and knew she'd have to work at trying to remain calm all the time. "Be right there," she said as she went and unlocked the door to let Scotty in.

"Morning Lily, you normally have the door open by eleven. You sleep in?"

"No, just got busy cleaning things up and didn't realize what time it was."

Scotty entered and began to take off his heavy coat, "Good God Lily! What happened to your face?" Then instantly he recognized that it had to have happened after hours, but instead he said, "Did one of those late night drunks hit you after I left when you were trying to close up?"

Thankful that he hadn't said J.D., Lily quickly said, "Yes, but it's okay now. Don't be concerned." Lily silently accepted that Scotty definitely knew who had hit her. Still determined to set her plan in motion she said to Scotty, "Can you cover the bar? I've got to go get the booze ordered right away."

"Sure Lily, no problem."

"I don't think J.D.'s feeling too good. He's still up in bed. When he gets up, just tell him I'm off to the trading post on the booze run."

"I'll do it."

Lily took her coat from the coat rack, stuffed the order list in her pocket and let herself out the front door of the saloon. The temptation to run was great, but she managed to control herself, as she hurried to her house to write a letter to Anna.

She took her skeleton key from her pocket, unlocked the door and let herself into the house. She found the writing paper, pen and ink, then sat down to write. "Dear Anna, You were right about J.D."….. She briefly outlined what had happened and the need for a steamship ticket to Seattle as soon as possible. She finished off the letter with, "I'll fill you in more when I see you, Love Lily," then put it in an envelope to be mailed. She put the letter in her pocket and hurriedly locked up the little cabin and left to mail the letter and pickup the liquor order.

Scotty was still behind the counter when Lily got back, and as she began putting away the liquor, she cautiously asked, "Is J.D. up?"

"Yeah, he's over in the barber shop. Looks a little rough around the edges. Guess he hard a hard night."

"I guess you might say that," and Lily thought to herself, guess I had a hard night too.

That early evening, as usual, J.D. closed the barber shop and came over into the saloon. After taking a seat at the very end of the counter, he looked at Lily behind the bar and said gruffly, "Give me a shot of whiskey. Make it the good stuff! Not that crap we give the customers."

Lily noticed he was slowly sipping at the whiskey, and began to wonder if he was trying to limit his drinking, or was he merely making sure that he had her under his control. Not that she had much time to think about it as it was the busy time of the evening and for the next four or five hours she had to wait on the customers. Typically, some were loud, some were good-natured, and some were quiet. No doubt thinking of the fortunes that they would make in the gold fields, or possibly wondering why they, like many others, had ever come to such a God forsaken place.

It was after twelve o'clock when the last customer left. Scotty stacked his chips and put away his playing cards, dumped out the ashtrays on his table, and was the last to go out the door. "Good night," he said stepping out into the cold and drizzling night.

J.D. was still at the end of the counter and he ordered Lily to pour him another shot of whiskey. As she turned to put the bottle back on the shelf, he spoke for the first time that evening. "Lily, sorry but I didn't mean to hit you that hard."

Lily noted that he wasn't apologizing for hitting her, just that he hadn't meant to hit her 'that hard'. She tried to make it easy for him and said, "Guess I just had too much to drink J.D. I know that you've gone out of your way to help me."

"Damn right I have! Glad you finally recognized that fact. Now you've got to remember that you're mine, and what I say around here goes."

"You're right J.D."

He was flushed with his own power and quickly downed his drink in one swallow then ordered, "Give me another shot." He felt he had won completely. It was almost too easy.

Lily continued to clean up after closing, wanting to delay as long as possible before going to bed, and then she got an unexpected reprieve as J.D. told her to, "Put the bottle on the counter, and I'll turn out the lights when I get done."

Lily did as she was told, then quietly left the room. She knew J.D. well enough by now. He would sit there and drink the entire bottle down before staggering into the bedroom. Then, if she were lucky, he would pass out again.

From here on the days and nights remained pretty much the same as Lily continued to acquiesce to J.D.'s more frequent drunken ranting and ravings. Some times when he came to bed he'd be looking for sex, but more often he would pass out. Each morning Lily would carefully get out of bed, being sure not to wake him, and go about the business of running the bar. So far, in spite of his demands during the day, she had been able to avoid being hit again, but she knew it was only a matter of time until it would be repeated.

She did not check on the mail's arrival at Bailey's because she knew it took about six to eight days for a letter to get to Anna. And then the same length of time for a letter to get back to Dyea. After twelve days she could no longer contain herself and began to check for mail every other day, except on the days when she knew that no ship had come in. She was getting desperate and didn't know how much more physical or verbal abuse she could stand if J.D. went on a rampage again.

Finally on the thirtieth of May, she got the letter from Anna. She walked to one side of the hotel and tore it open. Inside was a ticket for passage on the Al-ki, the same boat that she and Ben had originally come up to Dyea on. Lily was ecstatic. Good old Anna! She had come through in a pinch. She checked the date on the ticket. It was for June second. Two days away!

She suppressed her feelings, trying not to show how happy she was at this moment. J.D. could scream, holler, rant and rave, do anything he wanted. He couldn't stop her now. She stuffed the letter in her coat pocket and left to pick up six bottles of whiskey from the trading post before going back to the bar.

She was on pins and needles all day long on June the first, just trying to get through the day and not give anything away. It turned out that J.D. followed his normal routine, in fact he had even seemed to drink more that evening than usual.

The next morning Lily followed her careful, but usual routine, except that she purposely forgot to make the morning booze run. Scotty came in at his normal time and went right to his table to prepare for any poker players who might arrive early. At eleven J.D. finally got up, and ignoring Lily, made his way into the barber shop.

Lily had a knot in her stomach as she waited anxiously for the time to move while tending to the day's early customers. She knew the Al-ki would dock off shore about four in the afternoon, and she counted on being hidden in the mass of humanity that would result. At three in the afternoon she called over to Scotty, "Can you take care of these boys at the bar? I've got to make a quick booze run. I forgot about it earlier."

"Sure Lily, I've got it covered. Take your time."

She took a list of items needed to be purchased, stuffed it in her coat pocket and went out the door. "Thanks Scotty, I appreciate it."

Once outside she began the walk towards the trading post, but soon veered off and went directly to her cabin, unlocked the door and went inside. She pulled a chair to one side and stood on on it get the 'safe' out of the attic space. Quickly she took the money that remained and put it in her other coat pocket along with the ledger and the ownership papers to half of Bartlett's. She replaced the 'safe', closed the attic space, and put the chair back by the table. Then hurriedly packed a small suitcase with a very minimum of clothes, threw in her diary and walked out the door, on past the store fronts towards the shoreline.

The Al-ki was on time, possibly a bit early. She could see it off in the distance at the end of the small harbor, and already small boats were moving out to assist those coming ashore with their baggage and supplies. When the second wave of boats left to go back out to the steamer, Lily made sure she was on board. She tried her best to sink low in the flat bottom barge and be as inconspicuous as possible. Finally the barge pulled alongside the Al-ki and she immediately hurried to get on board. Upon reaching the main deck she found a spot between some deck cargo and the main cabin where she could wedge in behind to keep out of sight. She had come this far and didn't want to risk having J.D. or possibly one of his friends find her before the ship weighed anchor and left the inlet.

Anxiously Lily waited for the ship to leave the harbor, hoping no one would miss her. Or worse yet, come and start looking for her. Time appeared to move so slowly and she became more nervous with each delaying minute. She glanced at her watch, almost six o'clock. Then a blast of the ship's horn sounded, making her jump. Ever so slightly at first, the ship began to move out of the harbor. She was on her way at last!

On June eleventh the Al-ki arrived at the Port of Seattle after a slow trip with stops at Skagway, Vancouver Island, Anacortes, and Bellingham. Lily eagerly scanned the docks for a glimpse of her friend Anna, but was unable to locate her. Even though the sky was partly cloudy, she was in a good mood. She didn't have to worry anymore. She was free to do what she wanted, when she wanted. Her life was hers to live again.

The familiar skyline of Seattle was her domain and she could relax and breath freely. She took a big deep breath and walked down the gangplank. Anna was not to be found. Lily was not concerned because she knew that she could probably call Anna on the new telephone system that was now available in the Puget Sound area.

What to do first? She looked at her watch. It was early afternoon and since she was near the Rochester House on Pike Street, she decided to go there for a quick visit to see old friends. With her suitcase in her hand and everything else she owned in her pockets she was now ready to take on the world. A fast twenty minute walk brought her to the posh upscale restaurant.

She pushed open the door to see the same slight built clerk, Russell Jewet behind the front counter. Without blinking an eye, he looked up and said, "Welcome Miss Lily. Glad to see you again. Would you like a table?"

"No thank you, Russell. I'm just here to see Angelina for a minute, if she still works here."

With usual sense of politeness and correctness he answered, "Yes, she does. If you wait here, I'll go find her for you."

"Thank you, Russell."

Shortly they both returned to the front of the restaurant and Lily ran up to Angelina and gave her a big hug. "Oh, it's so good to see you again. It's been so long. It seems like years."

Nonplused, Angelina replied, "Well girl. It has been at least two or three years."

"Getting right to the point. Any chance that I might stay overnight with you? Someone was supposed to meet me on dock, but I'll have to call her in Tacoma later."

"Sure girl. I'm still at the same place, you know where it is. Is Ben with you?"

"No, I'll explain later," said Lily thankfully. "I'll head up to your place now. I don't want to bother you here at work."

"You go right on. You know where the key is. I'll see you after work."

"Thanks Angelina," said Lily as she turned to leave, but then she couldn't resist kidding Russell and said to him, "Really Russell, you should learn to smile more."

Russell P. Jewet stared back, not comprehending.

Lily found Angelina's hidden house key and let herself into the flat and dropped her small suitcase on the floor. What to do next was now the question? She decided to call Anna and make arrangements to meet her. Then, perhaps eat out, as Angelina would have already eaten at the Rochester House as usual.

Accordingly she left the flat and went to the nearest telephone exchange about three blocks away and made a phone call to Anna's house in Tacoma. Anna's younger sister June, answered the line and said that Anna would be coming up to Seattle on Monday the thirteenth to meet her. Lily then gave June, Angelina's address to give to Anna. After paying for the phone call she left the building.

Now, where to eat? She looked up and down the familiar streets of the city and decided she would take a stroll first and enjoy the hillside views of Seattle and the harbor area with its tantalizing smells and sights. She walked down towards the train depot, then along the waterfront and put her bare feet in the waters of the Puget Sound which she found delightfully clean compared to the muddy tidal flats of Dyea. Next, she found a new cafe on the waterfront that catered to the dock workers and finally had a late evening meal before heading back to Angelina's.

Back at the apartment, she was totally relaxed both mentally and physically as she took off her coat and shoes before laying down on the bed to await Angelina's return from work. At eight thirty she awoke as Angelina came home from her job. Lily looked up, "Guess I was more tired than I thought. I dozed off while waiting for you."

"Well girl, that's what beds are for. To rest, to sleep, whatever. Now that I'm here, tell me what's going on in your life. How long are you here for? Where's Ben? And what brings you down here? Where are you going? When are you planning on going back?"

"Oh, so much has happened since I left Seattle. I don't hardly know where to begin."

"Well, begin at the beginning," said Angelina as she sat down on a chair, took off her shoes and put up her feet up on another chair.

"To start with, a long time ago, you told me to watch out for men. Now I have to agree. One just doesn't know what can happen." Then she began explaining about Ben's good freight business in Dyea, how he got disenchanted and eventually got the gold fever and left. She told of working at Bartlett's and then later buying into the business, not realizing that all the while the owner was after her. She told Angelina about J.D.'s drinking and that she left because of it, but she left out a lot of the details about what she had gone through. That part was now over, and because she was wiser, it would never happen again.

Angelina took in every word. "You never heard from Ben again?"

"Not a whisper, not a letter, nothing."

"And if he does come back, do you think he would come looking for you?"

Lily paused, "I hope not. Before he left I began to see a different person. More moody, more set in his ways, more determined. I really think I might be afraid of him now."

"Men are just plain bad news girl. I tried to warn you. And speaking of warning you, there's someone around here that you'd best stay clear of."

"Who? I can't imagine who it would be."

"You remember that sly and sneaky Ron Appleton you went out with a few times?" Angelina questioned.

"Sure, but that was over three years ago!"

"That may be, but he seems to have gone off the deep end. Says you're the only woman who ever run out on him, and someday he is going to get even with you."

"What! I can't believe it!"

"Well girl, you'd best believe it, 'cause every time I see him around I hear him telling someone that he will get 'that bitch' and make her pay."

"I don't have any intentions of seeing him, and anyway he certainly doesn't even know I'm in town."

"Don't be so sure. I've heard he's so paranoid he even checks some of the passenger manifests on incoming ships for your name. I think he has a few crony contacts that he pays off for that information. Maybe buys them a beer or so, I don't really know for sure."

"This is absolutely absurd!"

"Well, as crazy as it sounds, I'd keep a eye out for him."

Angelina brought her up to date on other happenings around the Rochester House. The ex-detective P.J. Concannon still owned the business, but had been talking recently of possibly selling out and retiring to California. Katy, a waitress that had worked with Lily, had moved to Portland, Oregon to be closer to her family. Angelina told her of new buildings around town that had been built or sold. Most of which Lily had never heard of. Still, the two friends continued talking until long after midnight.

The Rochester House was closed on Sunday and that allowed both of the women to enjoy a leisurely morning and day together. They had a late brunch at Angelina's, then set out to cherish a warm sunny day, primarily window shopping as most of the stores were closed on Sundays. Even though Angelina was quite a bit older than Lily, they had a warm and comfortable relationship. Anna was Lily's confidant, but Angelina was like a big sister, a protector of her surrogate charge.

The end of the day brought the two back to Angelina's apartment with sore and aching feet, ready to be soaked in buckets of warm water. After heating water in Dyea on a temperamental wood stove, Lily enjoyed the pleasure of turning on the hot water tap and having instant hot water from a boiler hidden deep within the building. She also enjoyed the convenience of having electric lights. Civilization definitely had its pleasures, she decided.

The following day Angelina left for work right before eleven and Lily remained in the flat waiting for Anna's arrival. Shortly after one there was a knock on the door. "Lily? It's me, Anna."

Lily was drying some coffee cups by the kitchen sink. She put the dish towel on the counter and hurriedly opened the door. "Oh Anna, it's good to see you! Come in. I was wondering when you'd get in. I talked to June, but I didn't find out what time you were going to get here."

"Sorry I wasn't there to meet you when the boat came in, but I came down with a bad case of food poisoning Saturday morning. I was sicker than a dog all Saturday and Sunday. Couldn't even get out of bed. I wanted to call you, but of course there was no way to get hold of you on the boat."

"Food poisoning! What in the world did you eat to get that?" asked Lily.

"I really don't know. The only thing I could think of was tainted meat, or perhaps a salad. Anyway, I'm over it now, although I'm still a bit weak."

"Well, June didn't even mention it when I called your house."

Anna rolled her eyes, "That's June! She only remembers half of what anyone tells her. She seems to be off in her own little world most the time. But that's really not important now. What's going on with you? What happened up there?"

Lily filled her in on J.D.'s drunken behavior and how, with Anna's help of getting a ticket, she had fled from Dyea on the Al-ki. "I was so afraid at the last moment something would go wrong, and was I ever relieved when that boat began to move out of the harbor!"

"Well, you're safe here. What's your plan now?"

"According to Angelina, I'm not so safe here either.

"What are you talking about?"

"Take your coat off and sit down a minute and I'll tell you. Do you remember a Ron Appleton that I went out with a couple of times here in Seattle before I married Ben?"

Anna looked puzzled. "Only vaguely. You may have mentioned it, but I can't remember for sure."

"I only saw him a couple of times," Lily continued. "Now Angelina said he's gone kinda berserk and is looking for me to get revenge for dropping him years ago. Isn't that crazy?"

"Sounds crazy to me. Are you sure?"

"Sometimes I'm not sure of anything anymore. It really wouldn't surprise me that Ben might even turn up down here looking for me. He too, seemed to change before he left. Threatened to find me wherever I went."

"Lily, it seems like you can really pick 'em."

"I just don't understand how I could get all tangled up like this. Hey, let's change the subject. How much was that boat ticket you got for me?"

"Oh that. It was seventy-five dollars. I got it through my friend Clarence Emery. I told you about him before. He's got an office now in Tacoma, so I just called him."

Lily reached for her purse laying on the bed, "Please tell him 'thank you' the next time you talk to him, and thank you too." She opened her purse and began to count out the money on the table. "I really don't know what I would have done if you hadn't sent me that ticket. You helped get me out of that horrible place. I don't ever want to see it again"

Anna picked up the money and put it in her purse, then asked, "What are your plans now?"

"Right now, I need to look for a job and also figure out a way to get my money out of Bartlett's Saloon. You remember I told you I own half of it?"

"Yes, I do"

"I think it's worth about six thousand dollars. I brought the papers with me, but I don't know how I can get the money out of it from down here, and I certainly don't want to go back up to Dyea and meet that drunken sot J.D. again. I know I'm going to need some sort of legal help on this, that's for sure."

"It's beyond me too," said Anna. "but let me think about this for a minute or two." After a few minutes she said, "I think maybe I can help. I know two people that may be able to help, or if they can't, should be able to steer us to the right person."

Lily looked eagerly towards her friend. "Who do you know?"

"One is Clarence Emery. He is the one who got the boat tickets for us when we needed them, and he seems to have connections all over Seattle and Tacoma. The other is Mrs. Jenkins. She is the Secretary of States's wife, and she ought to be able to connect you to the Attorney General of the State of Washington. I would think that the Attorney General should be able to work something out with the authorities up in Alaska."

"Wow! That sounds great! How do you know these people?"

"They're both shirt tail relations to my father. I thought I'd told you about them years ago."

"I think you did mention one time that Clarence Emery was related, but I had forgotten that. How do we get a hold of them?"

Anna rose from the chair and began to pace, "Like I said, Clarence has an office in Tacoma. Possibly I can set up a meeting with you there." She paused to think though the problem. "Now I'm almost sure that Mrs. Jenkins, I don't remember her first name, has some sort of social function going on in Tacoma this week. I think with the mayor, or his wife, I'm not sure what it is. I just might be able to get you an opening to see her too."

"Oh Anna! I love you!" gushed Lily. "You're my life saver! What would I ever do without you?"

"Don't get too excited. Let me think. Today is Monday. I've got to get back to Tacoma right away and try to make these contacts for you. It wouldn't do a bit of good to try and make telephone calls from here. I'd be calling in the dark so to speak. Time is important, especially if we can get you an appointment with Mrs. Jenkins before she goes back to the State Capitol in Olympia."

"This is the best news I've had in a long time. Let me grab my stuff together and we'll get going!"

"I'd suggest you wait here. It might take three or four days, or longer, before I can make these connections. Why not wait here at Angelina's and use the time to look around for a job, in the meantime I'll try to set things up for you."

"I suppose you're right."

"Now, how can I get hold of you?" Anna looked around the room, "Angelina's apartment here doesn't have a telephone."

Lily thought for a moment, then replied, "Call the Rochester House and leave a message with Russell at the front desk. I'll check with him each day."

"That will work, I'm sure," said Anna while looking at her wrist watch, "My goodness, it's already after three. Time goes by so fast. I think I'd better be going right now. I'll try to catch the four o'clock train back to Tacoma and get started on this first thing in the morning."

Lilly rose and started helping Anna put her coat on, "I don't know how I can ever repay you. You're a gem."

"Oh I'll always remember that you owe me and that you'll always be in my debt," kidded Anna.

"Just the same, thank you," said Lily as the two exchanged parting hugs, "and good luck,"

The next morning Lily got out of bed early, being careful not to wake Angelina. She dressed and left a note on the small table saying she was out job hunting and would drop by to see her at the Rochester House later, then eased out of the apartment.

Once out on the street in front of the building Lily looked at a beautiful, totally clear, sunny June morning. If at all possible, a day to be thoroughly enjoyed in the northwest. However, her first stop was for a quick breakfast of eggs, coffee and toast at the corner cafe she had noted just three blocks up the street. She bought a copy of the Seattle Post-Intelligencer newspaper from a passing paper boy for five cents and proceeded to read the help wanted ads as she ate.

She was sure that she could go back to work at the Rochester House, but with that bizarre Ron Appleton around, she didn't want to add to any present problems. It would be better all around if she could find a job somewhere else. Then it would take more time for 'weird' Ron to find her if he was still so inclined. She was beginning to feel like her old strong self again.

The want ads didn't look too promising. Most of the ads were for men, and she knew that they would be quickly taken by those still trying to earn enough money to go to the Yukon gold fields. She rolled up the newspaper, put it under her arm, and after paying for the breakfast, left to begin her hunt for employment.

By late afternoon Lily's feet were aching from walking up and down the rough streets of Seattle. She remained confident, and even though she hadn't landed a job, felt very sure she had a couple of good leads to follow up on later.

The large clock outside the railroad depot read four o'clock. It was time to call it a day, but before that she decided to go up by the Rochester House to see if there was any word from Anna. It hardly seemed possible that there would be any message this soon, but she did tell Anna she'd check daily. She walked up Pike Street and twenty minutes later entered the restaurant.

"Good afternoon Miss Lily. I have a message for you from an Anna Baker," said the absolutely correct Russell Jewet, as he reached under the counter and handed her a note.

Lily read the paper. "Have set up a meeting with Clarence Emery in the Chilberg Restaurant at the Donnelly Hotel in Tacoma on Pacific Avenue tomorrow morning at ten. Mrs. Jenkins should be joining you about the same time. Good luck, Anna."

"Oh my," gasped Lily.

"Is something wrong, Miss Lily? asked Russell.

"Oh no, it's just that I didn't expect this news so soon." Lily recognized that there was no time to waste. She had to catch the train right away for Tacoma. She turned to go out the door, "Please tell Angelina that I had to leave for Tacoma right away. Tell her I'll call her later and fill her in. And oh, thank you," she added as she rushed out the door.

Lily almost ran to Angelina's apartment to gather up her things. How was Anna able to put all this together so fast, she marveled. Everything just seemed to fall into place. Now hopefully, she would be able to get legal help to sell her ownership in Bartlett's. That Anna had come through for her again! Again she wondered how she would ever repay her.

Shortly after Lily had left the Rochester House, Angelina came up to Russell at the front desk. "Was that Lily I heard up here earlier?"

"Yes, it was. She rushed out right after I gave her a message from someone named Anna about some meeting in Tacoma tomorrow morning. Said to tell you, she'd call you later."

"Well, that girl!" said Angelina somewhat indignantly "She didn't even take time to say goodbye."

They both turned to see the owner P.J. Concannon coming up to the front counter. "Angelina, has Lily come by yet" he asked.

"Came and left right after she got a message from Russell here."

"Damn," said ex-detective. "I checked around like you asked me to, and you were right. Some damned idiot is looking for her!"

"I tried to warn her," said Angelina.

P.J. looked to Russell, "Did you remember where she was going?"

"Yes sir, it was the Donnelly Hotel in Tacoma."

"Okay, let's see if we can send a wire to her care of the Donnelly. Russell, call a boy and have him come back to my office and I'll write out a quick message."

"Yes sir, Mister Concannon."

When the seven o'clock train for Tacoma left Seattle Lily was on it. She chose the cheaper second class seating, and once in her seat, when no one appeared to be watching, she carefully looked in her purse to count what money she had left. It was getting tight. She had paid back Anna for the boat ticket, bought food and now she would have to pay for lodging over night. She had heard of the Donnelly Hotel and knew that it was a costly place to stay and made up her mind to find a cheaper room for the night. She had to find a job soon, but she knew that she could count on Anna for a temporary loan if she had to have one. She'd made it through tougher times and she could certainly get through this time too she decided.

The train pulled into the Tacoma railway station a little before nine o'clock in the evening. It was still light out, but rapidly getting dark. After inquiring at the depot Lily was able to find a respectable room at the Sunrise Apartments on Commerce Street above Pacific Avenue for two dollars a night.

At five o'clock small rays of the Wednesday morning rising sun began prying their way past the curtains and into the small room. The Sunrise was aptly named Lily thought as she tried to remain in bed a while longer to get a bit more sleep. Realizing that sleeping any longer was a lost cause, she finally got up a little after six and proceeded to get ready for her morning appointment. It would hopefully be a fruitful day.

She carefully combed out her hair and lightly applied her make up, remembering the hair dresser in Tacoma long past, who told her to always use just hints of make up. Never overdo it. Next, she centered the small hat with the white bow on the top and fastened it down with two four inch long hat pins. She checked the outcome in a small mirror above the wall hung basin, and felt satisfied with the results.

It was eight o'clock when she checked out of the Sunrise with her small suit case and walked down to Pacific Avenue and into the Railroad Cafe, which obviously catered to the rail yards across the street. She ordered her usual coffee, scrambled eggs and toast, then sat back and ate a slow and leisurely breakfast. She had plenty of time before she had to meet Mister Emery at ten.

After taking all the time she thought she could without being obtrusive, she paid the bill, left the small cafe and began slowly walking towards the Donnelly Hotel and Chilberg's Restaurant. She felt it was important to be on time, but not too soon either.

It was easy to find the hotel as there was a large sign on the third floor level that loudly proclaimed in large white letters about five feet high, "Donnelly Hotel". As she approached the entrance of the building, a man of about forty years of age was walking towards her. They both arrived at the entrance at the same time. He reached for the door ahead of her and asked, "Are you per chance Miss Lily Chandler?" Lily stopped at the open doorway as he continued almost apologetically, "Oh, excuse me. I'm supposed to meet a Lily Chandler here at ten."

"Are you Mister Clarence Emery?" she asked.

"I am."

Lily gathered herself, "Yes, I am Lily Chandler. Nice to meet you. I thought I would meet you through one of the waiters inside," she smiled widely at him, "but this works just as well."

Mister Emery bent over slightly and waved her through the doorway and into the restaurant, "After you, please. May I help you with your suitcase?"

"Why thank you Mister Emery."

Mr. Emery took Lily's small suitcase and followed her into a large chandelier lit room with ornate curtained booths for private dining. Lily observed that this was certainly no cheap cafe. This was all top drawer without a doubt. Mister Emery waved casually to one of the approaching waiters, "Fred, a booth for me and the lady please."

"Right this way please, Mister Emery," said the waiter as he led them to booth number three and held the curtain back. "Will this be okay sir?"

"It will do just fine, Fred." Mister Emery looked at Lilly, "After you please." As Lilly entered the booth, he slid her small suitcase under the table and said to the waiter, "Please bring us a menu." Then he sat down across the booth from Lily. "Now, what can I do for you? Anna said you have a legal problem. I'm not sure I can help as I'm not an attorney."

There was a gentle tap on the outside of the booth and the curtain was opened. "I have your menus, Mister Emery," said the waiter. "May I suggest the fresh strawberries that are now in season, or perhaps you would like the full breakfast which is still being served."

"No thank you Fred, just something light for now. The strawberries sound good, possibly with cream. What do you think Miss Chandler?"

"Oh, I agree. That would be fine. Perhaps coffee too?"

Clarence Emery looked to the waiter, "Two bowls of strawberries with cream, and two cups of your fresh coffee, and I'll have cream for my coffee as well."

"I'll have the same," said Lily as she studied the man across from her. His light brown hair, although slightly receding, was neatly cut and trimmed as was his nicely groomed small mustache matched by a thin brown beard that came to a point at the end of his chin. He appeared to be quite successful to be sure, plus he had Anna and her family's recommendation.

She immediately began to explain her problem to him. "First off, thank you for seeing me, especially on such short notice. And please call me Lily, everyone else does. Oh, and I want to mention that we may be joined by the Secretary of State's wife, a Mrs. Jenkins, I believe."

"Yes, I recall that my niece mentioned that she would be here."

Lily opened her purse, "I have here a title to half of a business in Dyea, Alaska and I need......" Lily stopped talking as there was a disturbance in the next booth.

Suddenly the curtains to their booth were pulled opened and Lily gasped, "Oh my God! What are you doing here?"

The wild eyed man squeezed into the booth beside Lily, "Thought you could run away from me did you! You little tramp, I said I'd get you!"

The man was disheveled and unshaven. Lily could smell the strong odor of liquor on his breath. "Let's talk about this sensibly," said Lily, as she looked pleadingly over to Clarence Emery for help.

"Yes, let's all calm down and we'll work this out," said Clarence as he tried to pacify the sudden intrusion by this wild man.

The deranged man looked at Clarence through bloodshot eyes. "You keep out of this! It's between Lily and me," he screamed as he picked up one of the table knives next to one of the napkins and lunged at Lily with it. "You think you're too pretty for the likes of me!" He jabbed the knife into her cheek and blood began to flow out and down the side of her face. "Now, you're not so damn pretty!"

Clarence grabbed the intruder's arm and pulled it away from Lily's face. The crazed man reached inside his coat with his free arm and pulled out a 38-caliber hand gun and fired one shot into Clarence Emery's chest. A black powder burn suddenly appeared on his white shirt and a small bit of blood began oozing out.

Blood continued running down Lily's cheek and onto the white table cloth as she grabbed the gun and the man's wrist with both hands. With over powering brute strength, the man stood up and turned the pistol down towards Lily and pulled the trigger. The impact pushed her back against the booth, but she continued to use her hands to bend the man's wrist away. The table cloth was pulled to one side as water glasses, plates and silverware fell crashing to the floor. Lily continued to fight, getting one hand completely around the weapon and bending his arm backward. Finally she wrenched the gun out his grip and quickly turned the weapon at her assailant and fired two quick shots into his chest. She pushed him backwards through the curtains and tried to stand up, then yelled out, "I've got the gun! I've got the gun! Come and get it!" Dazed and weak, with blood dripping from her face and oozing from her chest, she fell back into the booth and ejected the two last bullets from the weapon.

Pandemonium now reigned in the restaurant. Someone screamed, "Call the police!" Another yelled, "Call a doctor!"

A well dressed lady, later determined to be Mrs. Jenkins, fainted at the cashier's counter and the owner of the restaurant, Mister Chilberg, promptly picked the woman up and took her into the main lobby of the Donnelly Hotel. A telephone call was subsequently placed to her husband, the Secretary of State for the State of Washington, who later came to pick up his wife.

After leaving Mrs. Jenkins in good hands, Mister Chilberg ran back into the restaurant side of the building just as Lily had yelled out about the gun. He ran towards the booth, stepping over the man who had fallen to the floor just outside the curtain. He pushed the curtain aside and took the weapon from Lily's hands just as she collapsed in the booth. Mister Chilberg yelled for two of his waiters who came and carried Lily into the Donnelly Hotel side to await medical aid.

Within minutes the yells for help brought two policemen who entered the building with their weapons drawn. People were still in shock as Mister Chilberg and the police tried to calm everyone down to determine exactly what had taken place.

As peace was being restored a doctor came rushing into the building and was ushered over to the victims. He checked the pulse of Clarence Emery. There was none. A quick glance told him the man on the floor was dead as well. He rushed to the hotel section to check on Lily. The amount of blood and his physical examination confirmed that she had just died.

Except for identification, the tragedy was over. The police asked the witnesses to help identify those involved. Both Mr. Chilberg and his headwaiter identified Clarence Emery. No one in the restaurant knew the other man and woman. They opened Lily's purse to establish her identity, then they opened the dead assailant's wallet, found a ticket for passage on the ship Rosalie from Dyea to Seattle, and read the name James D. Bartlett, Dyea, Alaska.

◆   ◆   ◆

"And that is the story as I remember it and reading about it," said the gray haired woman sitting on the bench. "Once again, how did you say you are related to Lily?"

"I'm Ben Chandler's great, great granddaughter."

"Oh, that's right. And why does this story interest you so much?"

The young woman gathered her thoughts and replied, "Number one, for history of the event about my great, great grandfather's first wife. You see, the way I understood it, Ben Chandler, came back from the gold fields and found out that Lily had left, so he came after her. He found out that she was in Tacoma and got there just after the murders. I understood he attended the funeral. I also heard that he tried to get her diary, but after hearing your story, I guess we can assume that is gone forever. Number two, and the main reason I'm interested, is because

Lily had the title to the business in Dyea in her possession when she died. Since Ben Chandler was her legal husband, he ended up with those papers. I knew that he had them for years, and before he died, he passed the papers on to my mother who gave them to me. I guess that makes me the heir to Bartlett's Saloon in Dyea. I heard that you knew more about Lily than anyone else, so I wanted to find out if you could verify the stories I've heard over the years. Now, I know all of it is true, so now I guess I'll be going up to Alaska. Probably hire an attorney in Skagway to represent me and try to get whatever inheritance is left from the business, land, or property."

The elderly lady remained seated, then said quietly, "I don't think that will be possible."

"Why? What do you mean?"

"I went to Dyea about twenty years, maybe it was twenty-five years ago. The town no longer exists. It is now completely grown over with new trees. Just like the Alaskan gold rush—it's over, gone. Only the outline of a few foundations are even visible. I'm afraid my dear, that it would be a wasted trip."

The great, great granddaughter of Ben Chandler sat still for a minute or two digesting what she had just learned. "Yet I don't think what I have found out is totally wasted. It is a great piece of family history that I can pass on to my children." Then she added thoughtfully, "Perhaps if your father had known more about what Lily had gone through, he would have tried more to help her."

References

#1. The Klondike Gold Rush, by Graham Wilson, copyright 1997, Wolf Creek Books Inc, Box 31275, 211 Main Street, Whitehorse, Yukon, YIA 5P7

#2. Klondike Women, by Melanie J. Mayer, copyright 1989, Swallow Press, Ohio University Press

#3. Klondike Fever, by Michael Cooper, copyright 1989, Clarion Books, 215 Park Avenue South, New York, New York 10003

#4. The Alaskans, by Keith Wheeler of Time Life Books, 541 North Fairbanks Court, Chicago, Illinois 60611

#5. The Daily Ledger, Tacoma, Washington, Thursday, June 16th, 1898

#6. The Seattle Times, Lily Chandler's Career, June 16th, 1898

#7. The Seattle Times, Three People Killed in Tacoma, June 15th, 1898

#8. Internet, The Klondike Nugget, June 10th, 1900, extracted 6/9/03

#9. Internet, A Guide to Dyea, Alaska, by Murray Lundberg, ext. 6/9/03

#10. Internet, The Chilkoot Trail, extracted 6/10/03

#11. Internet, Stampede Routes to the Klondike Gold, from The Klondike News, (Vol 1, No. 1), April 1st, 1898, extracted 6/9/03

0-595-31520-8